SECOND SIGHT

By the same author

Danger at the Doghouse
River of Secrets

SECOND SIGHT

Griselda Gifford

Andersen Press • London

First published in 2003 by
Andersen Press Limited
20 Vauxhall Bridge Road, London SW1V 2SA
www.andersenpress.co.uk

The right of Griselda Gifford to be identified as the author
of this work has been asserted by her in accordance with
the Copyright, Designs and Patents Act, 1988

British Library Cataloguing in Publication Data available
ISBN 1 84270 217 3

Phototypeset by Intype London Ltd
Printed and bound in Great Britain by
Mackays of Chatham Ltd, Chatham, Kent

Chapter 1

'Sit down, Joanna,' ordered Morgan the Gorgon –
otherwise known as Mrs Morgan, the Head.

She fixed me with her turn-you-into-stone stare.
'This is the third time this term Miss Snook has sent
you to me. I know you haven't been with us for
long but you appear to have set yourself up as class
clown. I gather the last thing on your mind is real
work – you prefer Art. This latest offering—' She
waved in the air my brilliant drawing of Sneaky
Snook as a boa-constrictor, swallowing the only
other new kid in my form, Josh, so only his head
showed, shouting 'Help!' You could tell it was Josh
because of his surprised-looking hair and glasses.
There was a balloon coming out of Snook's mouth:
'I am eating Josh becourse I am thik and he is
clevver.'

'It's true – she's nasty to Josh,' I burst out.

'I can't have my staff criticised by a child,' she
said firmly. 'And look at the spelling!'

I looked. It didn't look quite right.

'If you paid more attention you would learn to
spell. I am writing to your mother to ask her to come
and see me about you, Joanna.' Then she leaned
forward and pinned a smile on her face. 'We want

1

to help you, dear. I know you've only been here just over a month but you'll be leaving us for Elmdale next term. You'll find the going very tough in such a big comprehensive if you play the clown all the time ... ' She wittered on and my mind wandered. The Gorgon didn't know I'd be going home and back to my own school soon.

I had to stop Mum finding out I was in trouble. Since IT happened, she got upset very easily.

As if she could read my thoughts the Gorgon said: 'Of course, I have only met your mother once when she came with her friend. She said she'd had a car accident. Is she better now?'

'Better?' I faked a laugh. 'She's fine now – galloping around.' Mum was still on crutches from the car accident before Christmas, over five months ago, but I didn't want the Gorgon's pity. Also, I didn't want Mum involved in little chats with the Gorgon about my behaviour – she had enough to worry her as it was.

The Gorgon took her glasses off and stared at me – her little hedgehog eyes boring into mine. I stared back. My eyes are big and blue. 'Angel-face,' Dad used to tease me. 'But inside's a real little demon!' He and Mum would laugh. Remembering, I felt happy for an instant, then very sad.

The Gorgon was talking. 'You're not listening, Joanna. I said I wondered if your father could come along? I believe your mother said he was a long-distance coach driver but he must get home sometimes.'

I wasn't going to tell her that we'd left my dad when we moved. For one thing, her sympathy would make it real when it was temporary, it had to be. 'He's not here at the moment,' I said. I lowered my voice. 'We have to say he's a coach driver but really it's something secret – abroad. He's not allowed even to tell Mum about it.'

She stared at me, about to ask more questions and I wished I could melt through the door. I was saved by the buzzer going for the end of the day.

'Got to collect my little brother, Miss,' I gabbled, making for the door.

She gave a huge sigh. 'Don't disappoint me, Joanna,' she said.

I hardly heard her. Doddy would be waiting for me at his school, St. Matthew's Primary, round the corner. When Mum said she couldn't walk to collect him, his teacher had agreed to keep him until I came. He got all worked up if I was late.

I went across the square, past St. Matthew's church and Vicarage. There was a big notice on the Vicarage gate:

ST. MATTHEW'S CHURCH FAIR: Saturday,
May 29th
Stalls, Side-shows, Bring and Buy

The fair was tomorrow. Fairs made me think of the one that came to our village in Dorset. My little brother, Doddy, loved the rides and stalls. I'd take him tomorrow, while Mum got on with her work for her weird friend, Wendy, who owned our flat. Doddy hadn't talked properly since IT happened. I was always hoping that doing something he liked might change him back to normal.

St. Matthew's Primary faced the park and I thought I saw Josh, up by the bandstand, alone as usual. Doddy was waiting with Mrs Meek, his teacher. Although it was a warm day, he was muffled in his anorak with the hood up.

'Here's your sister, Donald.' Mrs Meek's voice was loud and cheerful – people talked to Doddy like this, now. 'Tell Mummy he's been very good today and painted her a picture. I wonder if your mother got my note asking her to come and see me, Joanna?'

I acted brain-dead, mouth slightly open. 'Dunno,' I said. I knew she hadn't because I'd opened it and thrown it away. *Donald has a few special problems that I think we should discuss*, Mrs Meek had written. Meaning, he acted like a robot, only doing things if anyone pushed him into it and hardly speaking. It seemed like he'd been this way for ever, only I got flashes of remembering how it was – before the accident. I hurried him away from the teacher before she said any more.

4

We always walked home across the park and now Doddy tugged his hand away and ran to the playground. As I hurried after him I saw several young kids – some with mums, plus the Three Thugs, Sara and her mates, Angie and Jackie. Nobody liked them. They bullied smaller kids at school, sometimes getting money off them. They were all massive and tried to look alike, with very short, bristly hair and a slouchy, don't care sort of way of walking. They were just sitting on the roundabout, talking and giggling and telling any young kids who wanted a go to shove off.

'Baby-minding as usual, Jo Jo!' Sara yelled at me as I came up. Doddy was running up to them and before I could get there, he tried to climb on the roundabout.

'Get off!' shouted Sara and when he took no notice she pushed off with her foot, deliberately making Doddy fall off. He screamed, clutching himself, and I saw the spreading wet patch on his shorts.

'Cry-baby needs a nappy!' Sara yelled. 'He must be six at least! He's mental like his sister!'

That's when I pulled her off and hit her. Then I was knocked over, kicked and someone sat on my back. I choked into the cork stuff, half-smothered, and Doddy was yelling.

The weight lifted, one of the girls screamed and Sara shouted, 'You can't hit a girl!' I staggered to my feet, hurting all over, and saw Josh chucking Angie over his shoulder with some kind of judo throw and he'd already got Sara hopping around holding her arm. Jackie was trying to hit him with her rucksack.

'You can't attack girls!' Sara shouted. 'I'm telling Miss tomorrow that you hurt Angie.' Angie was dead pale and dusting herself down, darting looks of hate at Josh.

'I don't care,' Josh said slowly, the way he always talked. 'I'll just tell how you pushed the little boy off.' He looked as tidy and unruffled as if nothing at all had happened. His face seemed bare and I noticed he wasn't wearing his glasses – just as well, perhaps.

I tried to calm Doddy, who was shaking and sobbing silently with huge gasps for air. 'You hurt my brother and I'll get my dad to sort you out,' I shouted before I could stop myself. 'He's big and tough – runs in the London Marathon.' Well, almost true – he was always saying he'd get into training for it.

'Yeah, yeah, we heard that before,' jeered Sara. 'He's not around, is he? And I can't help it if your brother's mental and deaf, can I?'

I ran for her, head down, ready to butt but someone gripped my arm.

'Leave it,' said Josh.

A fat woman was charging over to us from the

swings, a toddler on her enormous hip. Sensing trouble, Sara and her mates ran off. 'You big children didn't ought to be allowed in here – the little ones aren't safe.' Her face was red and enormous. 'That little boy' – she looked at Doddy, hidden in his hood – 'his mother didn't ought to let him out with rough kids like you. I shall complain.' She carried her toddler out of the fenced play area.

'She'll make trouble for us.' I didn't want Mum bothered.

'I don't think so,' said Josh. 'She doesn't know for sure which school we go to. Anyway, it was those girls.'

Doddy was clutching his knees and I saw that he'd grazed them. He pointed at a tiny smear of blood and went dead white. 'No, no, no!' he shrieked. 'No hospital!'

'It's only a scratch,' Josh said. 'He's a bit old to make such a fuss, isn't he?'

'No,' I snapped, hugging Doddy. 'He was in a bad car accident last year.'

'I like hospitals,' Josh said. 'I plan to be a brain surgeon.' He looked at me and added quickly, 'Were you in the accident too?'

'No and I don't want to talk about it,' I snapped. Then I added, 'But thanks for helping.'

'I saw you go into Morgan the Gorgon's. Was it that picture you did of Snook?'

'Sort of – and other things.'

'You don't need to stick up for me,' he said in a rather snooty voice. 'I can take care of myself. But it was a brilliant picture,' he added, more kindly.

Mum would be worrying and Doddy needed a plaster. 'Teatime,' I said to him but he sat down again and hid in his anorak.

'Isn't he hot in there?' Josh asked.

'He feels safer that way,' I said, trying to pull Doddy up but he'd gone all floppy. A limp five-year-old is heavy when you're a bit on the small side, like me.

'Watch me!' Josh suddenly shouted and did a handstand right in front of Doddy. Then he walked on his hands and threw in a quick cartwheel.

Doddy's head came out of his anorak like a tortoise out of its shell and I heard a strangled sort of hiccup. He was laughing!

Josh walked on his hands towards the playground gate and Doddy trotted after him. Right way up, Josh ran off, back the way we'd come. I wondered where he lived.

At last I managed to get Doddy across the park, to No. 26 Park Street, a gloomy terrace house where we lived in the basement flat. It belonged to Mum's old friend, Wendy, who had invited us all to stay as long as we liked. In return, Mum did some typing for Wendy, who worked for a company called Magic Make-up.

I wanted to get Doddy cleaned up while Mum

8

was still busy on her computer so I hurried him through the dark hall to the door of our flat. There wasn't a sound upstairs – Wendy must be out and I was glad. She was always popping in to talk to Mum or take her to one of her Positive Thought and Meditation Groups so I felt I'd sort of lost Mum as well as Dad. I suppose she tried to be kind but I thought if she'd not been around we might still be with Dad, rows and all.

We went down the steps to our basement door. I tried to sneak into the bathroom with Doddy but no chance. I reckon Mum can smell trouble. She was up from the PC and hopping across the floor with her crutches and into our little hall before I could move.

Doddy was sitting on the floor wildly sucking his thumb and holding his toy rat. He'd cuddled it so much that poor Rat had lost an ear and part of his tail. 'Doddy hurt,' he whimpered in the babyish voice that annoyed me, though I knew he couldn't really help it.

Mum put down her crutches and sort of collapsed on the floor beside him. She finds it hard to get up and down. Doddy, always ready for sympathy, began to cry again. 'It's only a little tiny scrape, darling,' she told him. 'Just needs a plaster. Oh dear, you've wet your shorts. Never mind, soon pop you into a nice clean pair.' She looked up at me. 'What happened?'

Life at school would be even worse if I told on the Thugs. 'He sort of fell,' I said.

'Nasty girls,' Doddy muttered.

'Someone pushed him?'

'Yeah.'

'And by the looks of it, you too, Jo?'

I knew she felt bad enough because she couldn't meet us from school so I quickly invented a scene so real that I believed it: 'I was on the swing and he was running around the playground with this little girl when she bumped into him and he went over. I got off so quickly that I fell over too!' I faked a laugh.

'You've a button off and a bruise on your face,' Mum said in a suspicious voice.

I knew my mum – crutches or not if she heard about Sara and Co. she'd be hobbling off to see their parents, baying for blood. 'Oh, my anorak got sort of caught up in the swing,' I said.

She dealt with Doddy's knee and I helped her up. Sometimes I got the supper because it took Mum a long time, balancing by the cooker, but today she'd made macaroni cheese and we ate it on the tiny table by the window. We had a good view of a wall and feet going past in the street. I tried not to think of our kitchen at home – where you could see right down the garden to the sea.

Doddy scrambled down to watch our mini TV.

Mum sighed and put down her fork. She'd left half her supper.

'Why can't I go and see Dad?' I burst out, as I had several times these last weeks.

Mum sighed. 'For a start, he'll be away a lot this summer taking tourists round Scotland – it's easier for him to stay with his friend Sandy in London between trips. Also, I want to get better and just think about the future. The accident put a strain on us.' She looked at me. 'You must have heard us arguing. As I keep telling you, Jo, I just want a complete break, to think things out. And I need to get more confidence walking. Wendy thinks she can help me there.'

She meant my dad couldn't help her and yet when he was home, he was always hovering around trying to cook or help in the house. I have to say his cooking wasn't very good and he left the kitchen littered with pots and pans but at least he tried. At first Mum had been grateful but later, it seemed to get on her nerves. This was when the rows began but always behind closed doors. If I came in, they would pretend to smile and one of them would go out.

That was what got me – I didn't know what the rows were about and I was almost certain that Mum started them. So it was totally out of order for her to leave Dad on his own – even if he was away part of the time driving his coach. I loved my mum but there was no way I could understand her at the moment.

Mum had some idea that Wendy's Group would help her and Doddy. It was true, she was getting sick of going to the hospital at home. The speech therapist didn't seem to help Doddy, either. They said it was the shock of the accident and he'd talk normally before long but at the moment, he could only manage to say about two words at a time. I sometimes felt kind of guilty that I'd not been in the accident too and yet I was glad I hadn't.

'Wendy really wants to help. She's lonely and we used to be great friends once,' Mum said. Wendy had been married three times but never had any children. I reckon this made her kind of bossy with Doddy and me. I could feel she was a bit scared of us in a way. Anyway, I know my mum and dad hadn't got on since the accident but I couldn't see it was a reason to leave poor Dad on his own. After all, it hadn't been his fault – Mum had been driving the car.

She now said she needed to get on with her work – Wendy would be back from her trip and asking for the typing. As she said it, I heard a car stop outside and I looked up, through the railings. Wendy's trendy black boots were clattering along the pavement to the front door.

Soon she'd be in our flat, saying, 'Am I interrupting anything?' with a silly sort of smile and

12

Mum would say, 'Of course not' and they'd look at the typing over mugs of coffee while I had to play with Doddy – and keep out of the way.

I wished hard that something would happen to change everything back to our old ways at our dear little cottage. Afterwards, I wondered about that wish . . .

Chapter 2

Sara and the Thugs were prodding me with hard fingers and I was tied up so I couldn't move or shout . . .

'Jo!'

I jolted awake to find Doddy on my bed, prodding me with a felt-tip pen. 'Stop it!' I yelled, pushing him away so hard that he bumped to the floor. He lay, crying noisily.

'Ssh – you'll wake Mum,' I said but it was too late. I heard the thud of her feet as she got out of bed next door and then the shuffle of her crutches. She slumped to the floor and clutched at Doddy. 'What happened?' She looked at me accusingly. 'I was working till late and now you've woken me at six!'

Doddy pointed at me. 'Jo cross!' he said accusingly. So of course she went on at me for shouting at him and then she saw the rash of red spots on the big white tee shirt I sleep in and asked me why I'd let him do that and I ought to know how difficult it was to get clothes washed and dried in the flat. And then, worst of all, she cried. Mum hardly ever cried. Doddy, sucking up as usual, patted her tenderly and I stared, feeling awful and wanting to kill my baby brother.

And it was Saturday so I couldn't escape to school.

I made some tea and things calmed down a bit but it wasn't the best moment to ask about going to the church fair. At breakfast I pushed my porridge round the plate – Mum said it was cheap and good for us but I remembered the happy crunching of Coco Pops – Dad used to snatch the packet first if he was at home.

I opened my mouth to ask Mum if I could take Doddy to the fair when she asked me if I could get some shopping. 'And could you take Doddy, love? I still have some urgent work to do for Wendy's Conference.'

It was 'love' these days when she wanted me to do something and Joanna when she was mad at me. 'OK,' I said. Why ask her about the fair? She'd probably say 'no' because of Doddy getting lost or something and anyway, she was back at the PC now, mouse in hand, peering at the screen with a worried frown. Last week Doddy had turned the computer off and she'd lost some work she'd forgotten to save.

'We'll give you a bit of peace, Mum,' I said. 'And have a walk in the park after shopping.' Well, we'd have to go through the park to get to the Vicarage garden.

'Don't let Doddy out of your sight,' she said. 'And there's breakfast to clear first.'

This took ages as Doddy would wash up, standing on a stool. Mum said it gave him confidence but he was a real pain, leaving bits of gummed-on porridge so I had to do the dishes again.

By the time he'd gone to wee, then changed into his little track shoes and the anorak he would wear whatever the weather and hunted for Rat, I thought we'd never get there. I brought his old buggy with me – after the accident he seemed to get tired quickly and want to sit in it, though of course he was too big. It was useful for shopping, too.

We'd just got outside our door when a familiar voice said, 'Taking little Donald out, Jo?' Wendy, who must be about six feet tall, was swooping across the hall. I wondered what her face was like under all the Magic Make-up.

I was tempted to say, 'No, we're not going out. I'm going to wheel Doddy up and down your hall,' but instead I grinned feebly and tried to get to the front door.

She fluttered her false eyelashes. 'Could I have a word?' she asked, like the people do in TV soaps. I nodded – as long as it was one word only! 'I wonder if you could turn down your pop music in your bedroom, Jo dear? Last night after I'd left your flat – it was particularly loud. I need an oasis of peace in the evening.'

16

As I said I was sorry I tried to remember what an oasis was and a vague picture of palm trees and Wendy sitting on a camel made me hide a giggle. 'It was a top group,' I explained. 'I'm drummer in a group at home ...'

'The Ravin' Rats,' Doddy said unexpectedly. Maybe he was getting a bit better.

Wendy looked concerned. 'Better to look to the present, now, Jo, and make new schoolfriends.' I thought of the Three Thugs. 'And all this pop music can't be good – no wonder children today can't concentrate.' She leaned over me, wafting great gusts of Magic scent over me. 'I wonder if you'd like to come with Mummy to one of my Meditation Meetings? It might help you to cope with your new life here. I know things are hard for you right now.'

Well, I suppose she was trying and maybe it was a great honour to be asked but did she realise not many girls of twelve want to meditate? 'I'm not very good at staying in one room for long,' I muttered. 'It's since the accident. It's called claus ... something.' This wasn't really true but at least Wendy's feelings wouldn't be hurt. 'Got to go,' I said quickly before she could give me her shopping list. She said she never had time to shop. Wendy always wanted weird things – herbal tea, strange vegetables and other things like tofu and funny rice with bits in it – which meant going to different shops.

We'd not been here long but already I was so

homesick: I missed Dad most of all, then our cottage, my bike and my pop group, the Raving Rats. I played drums on a second-hand set Dad had bought for me and him – that's if he didn't want to play. The Rats – Mikey, Karen, and Sam, our lead singer – would be practising without me and I'd be totally forgotten. We'd already had a couple of gigs – playing at schoolfriends' parties – and hoped for more.

Doddy would pick up things we didn't need and chuck them into the trolley so it took a bit of time to sort him out and it was getting late by the time we got to the Vicarage. It was another warm day. I got so hot I put my rucksack and a plastic bag, stuffed with shopping, on the buggy. I'd had a job to persuade Doddy he couldn't sit on top of them.

Children of five and under were free but I had to spend ten pence just to get in. I looked round for the fair. No roundabouts, no helter-skelter, no shooting for pink, woolly animals – nothing but boring stalls, a Bouncy Castle and a couple of small tents labelled CAKES and REFRESHMENTS.

Suddenly Doddy pulled me along to a stall covered by all sorts of rubbish – ancient radios, bits of china, ornaments, old lampshades. He darted ahead of me so he was out of sight.

I charged through the crowd after him. 'Stop pushing!' someone said irritably but I didn't care. I had to get him.

There he was, staring at bits of ornaments near the edge of the table – just at his eye-level. The sun was glittering on two round, flat, glass circles, so they sparkled invitingly. I'd just time to make out they were like eyes: dark blue with a black ring in the centre, circled with white, when Doddy's small hand snaked out and grabbed one of them. At the same time another bigger hand shot out from behind the woman next to me and snatched at the other glass thing.

They must have been joined together – Doddy pulled and yelled – the other hand pulled and Doddy bounced back into my arms.

The old bat in charge of the stall reared up from rootling amongst boxes. 'Put them back at once!' she snapped.

I unclenched Doddy's fingers and prised out the glass thing. A thin piece of broken chain dangled from it. 'There's only one – someone's nicked the other one.'

'Look in his pocket!' she ordered.

Doddy hid in his anorak hood.

'He's not got it!' I shouted. People were staring at us and the old bat looked as if she might explode.

'What's the matter, Amy?' A man dressed as a clown, face paint and all, came up to her.

Doddy stopped crying and jerked his head, like a tortoise out of his anorak-shell, to look at the clown.

19

'This boy's taken one of those foreign glass eyes Joshua gave us.' The old bat gave a look at Doddy which rivalled Morgan the Gorgon's.

'He didn't! Someone else did!' I yelled. 'And I'll pay for this one!'

I'd been going to chuck it back and leave the crappy stall but I wanted to show them I'd got money – we weren't just kids who nicked things.

The clown was looking at me. 'Haven't I seen you before? I know, St. Matthew's Middle School. You were the one at the back who asked the difficult questions.'

I stared. We'd not had a clown at the school! 'RE class – just after I came here, two weeks ago,' he went on, his clown's red lips smiling.

'Oh – you're . . .' I began.

'This is our new Vicar, Mr Johnson.' The old bat made it sound as if he was Royalty or something and I should bow.

He smiled at her. 'I'm quite sure that this girl's speaking the truth. Besides, they're only souvenirs from our trip to Turkey last year – Joshua insisted on buying them. They say the eyes bring good luck. I don't believe in magic charms and it seems he doesn't either, now – he insisted on giving them to the fair. I think five pence for a single eye, don't you?' He said it quite pleasantly but firmly. I gave her the money and she looked at me like I was dirt but she took it. The clown (I couldn't think of him as a Vicar) said he'd better get back to selling ice creams before they melted.

I dragged Doddy away. So Josh was the Vicar's son. He never said – but probably the class would have taken the mickey even more if he had. It wasn't just Snook who hated him for knowing all the answers and then going silent when he was bored.

'Let's see,' I said when we were clear of the crowd. Doddy opened his palm reluctantly. The Eye didn't really look much like one. No wonder Josh got rid of tacky tourist rubbish like that. 'I'll put it safe with the shopping,' I told Doddy and I zipped it up in the front pocket of my rucksack.

Doddy forgot the Eye and dragged me over to a man dressed as a pirate. There was a sheet of cardboard painted like sea with a desert island in the middle – I could have drawn better palm trees – and you had to write your name on a flag, attached to a pin, and stake your claim to treasure. Doddy got excited and jiggled around while I wrote his name and address on the label. While I was explaining about the treasure and trying to stop him putting the pin right in the middle of the sea (though I suppose there could be a sunken galleon full of gold), Josh came along, carrying dripping cornets. 'Dad said you'd bought an Eye,' he said. He held out the ice creams.

'How much?' I asked.

'On the house,' he answered in the grown-up way which got him teased. 'My payment for helping Dad.' He pointed and I saw the clown across the garden with a queue in front of him. 'It might not be so bad with one Eye,' he said. 'And maybe it won't work with you. Don't say I didn't warn you.' He looked seriously worried.

'What are you getting at? It's only a tourist thing, isn't it?'

'Most of them are – but these Eyes are different. It's the middle, the pupils – you can see through them and beyond and ... Well, I can't explain. It might not happen to you. It was dead weird, scary – I saw much more than I wanted. You'd not believe me if I told you ... Oh, there's Mum coming – I'd better go or she'll have me helping with the teas.' He ran off.

By now Doddy had put his pin in a palm tree and was off to look at the Bouncy Castle. As I ran to catch up with him I told myself Josh was just making it up.

The Bouncy Castle was full of little kids – I felt a right idiot going on it but Doddy dragged me and it was almost the first time since the accident that he'd got excited. I put the laden buggy by the Castle and watched it while we bounced. There was a shriek behind us. I pulled Doddy away just before I was thrown on the heaving floor. Small children were jumping off in alarm, Doddy was yelling and

Sara laughing. 'Shouldn't get in the way, you nerd!' she shouted.

I wobbled up and made a dive at her leg clutching at one of her ankles but she was pulling me off. The man in charge of the Castle was shouting but Sara made for the buggy and my shopping. 'Leave it alone!' I yelled. This was a big mistake because it made her even keener.

'What you got in there?' She was just going to open the zip when I head-butted her.

There was big trouble then – Sara wheezing and trying to get her breath – making a mega-fuss and Doddy crying, alone on the Castle. It wasn't fair – the man in charge went on at me while she nipped off. I'd had enough. I collected Doddy, picked up the rucksack and pushed the buggy out of the gardens. There'd been enough trouble for one day.

Doddy cried so much that I let him have his Eye back to hold. My watch said it was one-fifteen. Mum would be going ape.

When we came into the hall, Wendy was coming out of our flat. 'Your mother's been worried because you're late.' She put her hand with its rings as big as knuckle-dusters and long red-painted fingernails on my arm and spoke in a soothing, irritating voice. 'Now, Joanna dear, I know how difficult it is for children to understand grown-ups at your age but your mother needs all the peace of mind she can get if she's to walk properly again.'

'I am nearly thirteen,' I said, trying to sound dignified and not just cross. 'Mum knows she can rely on me.'

Doddy, bored with the talk, waved the Eye at Wendy. 'Look!' He held it out. Wendy obviously thought it was a gift and took it. 'Mine!' Doddy said.

'I'll give it back to you, dear.' She examined the Eye. 'I've seen these in Turkey. They're to ward off evil. Sometimes they paint eyes on the prows of boats as well.' She held it up to her face and Doddy looked as if he might cry. Then she gave a gasp. 'I thought I saw something! No – of course not. It's just thick glass in the middle.' She handed it back to Doddy so quickly that he dropped it on the tiled floor. 'Oh dear – I hope it's not broken,' she said.

Doddy picked it up. 'Poor Eye!' he wailed.

I saw the crack across it and then Mum called from our flat. 'Is that you, Jo?'

All the time I was longing to look in the Eye but Mum was hugging Doddy as if he'd come back from a space flight to Mars and told me I'd no consideration and where had we been?

I decided not to invent anything this time so I said, after shopping, to the fair at the Vicarage. I thought something to do with the church might sound OK. And I counted out her change. I'd only spent twenty pence of it – the rest was my money. It wasn't fair: she'd never have gone on like this before the accident. She worried so much that I had to be Saint Jo, instead of arguing back like ordinary Joanna Murray.

The stuff in plastic bags was all right but maybe the rucksack hadn't been a good idea – some things were a bit squashed or melting.

'Really, Joanna!' Mum said crossly.

Doddy's favourite and almost main food is bananas and he looked sad when he saw that two had burst their skins. 'Look – lovely mashed nana,' I said to him, trying a bit of Wendy's Positive Thinking.

'What are you clutching in your hand, love?' Mum asked Doddy but he ran off to our room.

She was getting lunch – muttering that the baked potatoes were overdone now – and I'd just put the shopping away when I heard Doddy make a strange crowing noise.

'See if he's all right, Jo,' Mum said.

I found Doddy crouched on the floor, staring into the Eye.

First he laughed, then squeaked: 'Go away! Nasty!' and dropped it. I snatched it up and put it up to my right eye. My heart thudded when I saw a kind of film running but sort of out of focus. I could only see part of a room; a corner of a stove, a shadowy cupboard. Was there some sort of tiny TV in the Eye? But how could there be? There were no switches, no wiring, nothing. I'd heard of people spying on others through some sort of Web link and computer cameras but they were complicated and expensive, not for sale at the church fair for five pence!

The crack in the Eye seemed to bend the room in a weird way. Suddenly I could see a man and woman, angry faces, mouths open but I couldn't hear the sound. And there was a boy – I decided it was a boy – reaching out a hand to something on the kitchen table, amongst a litter of bottles and half-filled glasses. The Eye glittered in the light. My view enlarged, like a camera close-up, and I saw it was the other Eye! Somehow it was clear and glowing, even though everything else was a bit fuzzy.

Before the boy could reach the Eye, the woman deliberately swiped her arm over the table, knocking the bottles, glasses and Eye to the ground. Her face was twisted with anger as she turned and slapped the man's face.

I saw his hands shoving her and as she fell both of them went out of the picture. The boy picked the Eye out of the mess of broken glass and liquid on the floor and ran up dark stairs and into a small room with peeling wallpaper and a bed. The view panned down to his shaking hands and I saw he'd cut the right forefinger as he held the Eye up to his face. Then everything went out of focus and I am reeling – dizzy – as the room vanishes and I am the boy, battered by angry thoughts so fast I can hardly catch them. One thought is clear: *I hate Mum and Dad!*

I tried to beam a thought back: 'Who are you? Where are you?' but Mum's voice made me jump.

'Whatever are you doing, Jo? And what's the matter with Doddy?'

I put down the Eye and saw her, balanced in the doorway. Doddy had burrowed his face down under the duvet, the wrong way round so his dirty bare feet were on the pillow.

'Just looking at one of Doddy's toys,' I said quickly. I pulled back the duvet before he could smother himself. 'You're OK, aren't you, Dod?'

'Noeye, noeye!' he muttered, sucking his thumb furiously, Rat in hand.

'He's talking a bit more, even if it's nonsense,' Mum said. She got herself across the room and down on her good knee to look at the Eye. I held my breath. Would she see anything through the Eye? She picked it up. 'Just a glass ornament. I suppose it's meant to be an eye. Do you want it?' She held it out to Doddy but he went back under the duvet.

I heard a bang on our door and Wendy knocked and immediately walked into the flat as if she owned it – well, I suppose she did. 'I wonder if you've finished my letters, Lizzie dear? You look so pale. Why not try my Magic Make-up? It's Organic so it can't harm your skin.'

27

Mum sighed. 'There's not been time. I've been too busy doing the other typing.'

The stones in Wendy's rings caught the light as she put both hands on Mum's shoulders and said, quietly, 'I'm sorry. Perhaps I give you too much to do but I thought it might keep your mind off things.'

Of course Mum smiled and said she was glad to do the typing and she was looking forward to the Meditation Meeting. This was the trouble with Wendy: I was just ready to hate her when she changed from Bossy Wendy to Kind Wendy. Which was the real Wendy?

All the same, I was glad when Wendy refused Mum's invitation to share baked potatoes and baked beans. 'Thank you, but I never eat anything out of a tin. I'm having mung beans and tofu today.'

As we sat down to eat, I couldn't help giggling. 'She's such a weirdo.'

Mum was helping Doddy with his potato, as if he were a tiny kid. If she went on like this he'd get more and more helpless. She looked up at me. 'Not a weirdo, Joanna – a great many people share her views. And she's very kind. She's certainly helping me to pull myself together and get away from everything that reminded me of the accident.'

'You mean away from Dad.'

'We were quarrelling a lot, darling. You know we were. I was making him unhappy, too.'

Because the accident was all her fault.

28

There was a ring at the front door and I heard Wendy going to answer it. Then she called through our door, 'There's a *boy* waiting to see Joanna.' She sounded as surprised as if a gorilla wanted to talk to me. I went up the stairs to the hall with Doddy behind me.

'Thought you weren't ever coming,' said Josh. He waved an envelope. 'Your little brother's won the the Treasure Hunt: two free tickets to Sevenstones Zoo!'

'Mine!' Doddy said, snatching at the envelope and running back to the flat, chanting, 'Doddy won! Doddy won!'

'Thanks for bringing them,' I said.

'See you at school,' he said, grinning.

'This Eye I've got. Tell me more about it.'

He turned round and his expression changed. He looked watchful, guarded. 'I said you wouldn't like it.'

'I can see things through it. Like a sort of spy camera. How does it work?'

'I wish I knew,' he said. 'I thought maybe it wouldn't be the same for you. And you've only got one Eye. With two Eyes you can see ... far too much.'

'I thought the Eyes kept evil away or something,' I said.

He gave me another strange look. 'They show you things that are wrong but you have to do the work. For instance – I saw my granpa lying on his floor, looking funny. I tried to tell my parents but they wouldn't believe me and said they'd just talked to him that evening. Well, we got a phone call to say a neighbour found him next day and he'd been lying in the cold all night.'

Jo felt a shiver go down her spine. 'Did he die?'

'No – but he got pneumonia. If they'd listened ... And it wasn't just that. I saw too much, heard too much. I felt I was going mad.'

I wanted to hear more but Mum was calling me and Josh said he had to get back. 'I shouldn't have put the Eyes on the stall but I thought they only worked for me,' he said, looking worried. 'If you keep the Eye, don't look through it. But I can't warn the person who took the other one.'

I went back to the flat wondering if I ought to throw the Eye away. But I felt drawn to it, in some weird way. It was like seeing part of a horror film. You just *had* to see the end even if it was scary.

Chapter 3

Mum wasn't excited by Doddy's prize. She said she couldn't walk round a Zoo on crutches and we were too young to go on our own – especially as it was a couple of miles away. Anyone would have thought I was Doddy's age! I said I could easily take Dods by bus but she said she'd ask Wendy if she'd very kindly take us there and pick us up, on Saturday when she was less busy.

'Gross!' I exploded. 'I don't want to go with her and she won't want to take us. You used to let me and the Raving Rats go off to the town on the bus. I can't help it if you've lost your bottle.' Doddy didn't help because he kept chanting, 'Zoo now!' as if he was about two years old.

Mum looked stricken and I felt awful. I told Doddy to shut up and hugged her. 'Sorry,' I said. I felt as if I'd been saying sorry ever since we arrived.

I had another look through the Eye when Doddy was asleep. This time, all I saw was darkness.

Next day was Sunday – I hated Sundays at Grunge House because I remembered Sundays as they used to be: sometimes going to church, then a special big lunch or in the summer a picnic – or

Dad and I would go for a long explory walk. And later, I'd have the Raving Rats round for a practice.

Guess what? On Sundays *here* it was a bundle of laughs – I had to do the ironing and keep an eye on Doddy while Mum went off to meditate and positive think with Wendy's group. Mum said I had to earn my pocket money now as we were poor. Well, we were poor because she'd left Dad, weren't we?

I left Doddy making a den for Rat on his bedroom floor and went to iron in front of the telly in the living room. I usually watched TV as I ironed – sometimes scorching things. Today Dad filled my thoughts. He'd only been driving for this London-based coach company for a couple of months, taking tourists on two-week holidays in Scotland. He'd lost his last driving job where we lived, in the West Country, when the coach firm went bust. He'd been out of work for months when he heard from his old mate, Sandy, about a job driving coaches on special trips to Scotland.

He and Mum were celebrating the new job before the accident. I remember seeing the bottle of wine on the table when Dad and I came back after that first terrible visit to hospital. Wine gave Mum a headache so she'd only have a small glass – so what really happened to make her drive into the back of a van?

I thought about London, only about forty miles

away from where we lived now. Why not just ask Mum for his address? I tried to work out when he'd get my letter. He'd been due home for a weekend just after we left. Then he'd be off for two weeks driving the coach round Scotland. I remembered now – he'd planned a weekend at home at the beginning of June: Mum and Dad's wedding anniversary. Mum had looked funny when he said that. I suppose she was already planning to walk out. Anyway, if I'd worked it out right he'd be at Sandy's in London this Friday night. Maybe he'd been ill and that was why he'd not written.

Doddy was screaming! I ran into our bedroom but he wasn't there and the door was open into the hall. Wendy was holding him as he tried to kick her ankles. Bewildered members of the Meditation Group were coming in the open front door.

'Leave him alone, you stupid cow!' I shouted and began to tug at Doddy, who yelled even louder, pulled between us like a worm between two blackbirds. Then Mum came hobbling up the short flight of stairs from our flat.

'Stop it!' she shouted and we both dropped Doddy so he skidded across the tiles.

'I caught him running off, down the pavement,' Wendy said. 'He could have got run over.' I saw now she was panting and looked upset.

'Joanna – I told you to watch him!' Mum said with gross unfairness.

'Find Dad!' Doddy sobbed and now I saw he'd put on his anorak and had one arm through his school bag. 'Run away!' he sobbed.

Mum hugged him. 'Apologise to Wendy at once for being so rude, Joanna.'

Suddenly I was sick of everything. 'I won't! I want to run home too. I want Dad!' I ran back to our flat and into the bedroom. I pushed Doddy's toy box against the door and flung myself on my bed.

Mum banged on the door and tried to push it open but I took no notice. To my surprise, she gave up at once and I heard her talking to Doddy and then clattering in the kitchen as if she'd forgotten about me.

Well, if she felt like that I wouldn't come out at all! I knew I was behaving badly and probably hurting her but I didn't care.

I thought about playing my tapes or reading but I felt sad and restless. Something drew me to take the Eye from under my pillow. At that moment I had the weird feeling someone was watching me – but nobody could see into a basement room!

A strange force compelled me to look into the black pupil of the Eye. Then I was deep, deep in a dark pool and a bigger unhappiness than mine wrapped round me, almost sucking me in. I could see a corner of a bedroom. The same boy sat hunched on the bed, with his hands over his eyes. A rough bandage was tied round his cut finger.

34

Although I couldn't hear anything his shoulders were moving as if he were crying. What was happening? How could I see into someone else's house? I felt sick with the strangeness of it all.

After a moment I couldn't bear it any longer and I pushed the Eye back under my pillow. Black sadness pressed round me until I felt almost smothered.

'Jo Jo.' Doddy was calling me softly. 'Doddy want Jo Jo.'

I rubbed my tears away and unblocked the door. Doddy ran in and hugged me. This was one of the times I loved my little brother very much.

I found Mum sitting at the kitchen table, beating a batter mixture to death. I was just going to explain that Doddy seemed to be playing happily earlier and I had no idea he was planning to run away, when she spoilt it. 'You were very rude to Wendy,' she said.

Then I exploded again. 'Wendy, Wendy, Wendy – I'm sick of her!' I shouted. 'You like her better than us, better than Dad! Give me Dad's address in London. I'm going to write to him even if he doesn't bother to write to us. I want to go home! This place isn't making you better, it's making you worse.'

Mum stopped beating. 'Stop shouting at once, Joanna. This doesn't help me at all. Of course I love you both best (I noticed she didn't say anything

35

about Dad) but Wendy is an old friend who wants to help. And there are complicated and grown-up reasons why I've left your father. There's a lot you don't know. You are too young.' She got up with difficulty and propping herself awkwardly against the stove, poured the batter mixture into the pan of sizzling sausages. 'I want you to apologise to Wendy. After all, if she'd not followed him, Doddy could have run in the road and been knocked down by a car.'

Doddy had been talking to Rat and feeding him with bits of cheese which he ate himself afterwards. Now he said: 'No car!' in a scared voice, so Mum hugged him.

'OK – I'll apologise,' I said grudgingly. 'But I want Dad's address. Why can't you tell me all about it? I'm not too young. Why hasn't he rung up or written?'

She didn't look at me. 'I expect he's busy. And we went off so quickly.'

'You didn't leave our address, did you, Mum?'

She went white – really white like people do in stories. 'I left a note to say I'd be in touch and we were staying with Wendy.'

'But he doesn't know where Wendy lives, does he?'

'No,' she said quietly.

I felt anger bunch up inside me and burst out: 'Dad's been worrying about us for a whole *month*!

I hate you! It's all your fault – your fault you were driving badly! Dad's done nothing!'

Doddy was staring at me. Then he made car noises and gabbled in a high, scared voice, something that sounded like, 'Sloal, goslo!' Then he began to cry and Mum and I both rushed to comfort him.

Mum kept on saying she was sorry and crying silently. I wasn't sure if she was apologising to me or to Doddy but I hugged them both and said I was sorry too. My fiery ball of anger had exploded and left me empty and sad.

'I'll apologise to Wendy,' I said. 'She does try to help.'

Mum looked up and smiled. Her face was a mess of red eyes and tear-streaks. 'Thank you, darling. Could you tell her I'll be up as soon as I've settled Doddy and put on a mask of Magic Make-up!'

Chapter 4

I thought about Dad all the way to school next day. I could see that no amount of nagging would make Mum tell me his address at Sandy's herself. She just wanted to cut off from him completely. I'd have to search through her things when she was upstairs. Usually, I'd never do that. Mum and Dad don't pry into my things and I leave theirs alone, too.

Doddy had made a fuss at bedtime so I'd given him the Eye back. He didn't try to look through it, perhaps because he'd been too scared last time, and I easily persuaded him to leave it at home in case it was nicked at school. Winning the Treasure Hunt had made him just a bit more confident and he actually went into school without crying and with his head out of his anorak hood.

'Tell them about your prize trip,' I called after him and he turned round and did a thumbs-up sign. Perhaps it might make him try to talk. I thought of the time before the accident. He used to drive me mad chattering and asking questions about everything. I'd have given anything for him to be like that now.

I went to dump my PE gear in my locker but I

was so busy thinking that I didn't notice the crowd of kids round the Three Thugs in the changing room.

'Here she is! Poor Jo Jo! Her brother's mental and her mum's a cripple! We got to be nice to poor old Jo.'

No prizes for guessing it was Sara chanting with Angie and Jackie joining in. Everyone laughed. I could have killed Sara. How had she found out about Mum? I knew she was winding me up on purpose and it was working.

'So what?' I said loudly but my voice wobbled with anger. 'OK – my mum and brother were in a car accident but they're both getting better.' I noticed some of the kids stopped laughing.

'Some accident! I bet they've been like that always!' Sara yelled.

I charged her with my games kit and it took her by surprise. For a moment she was pinned against the lockers. Then her jumbo Minders leaped forward and knocked me down. The changing-room floor was hard and I felt blood dripping from my nose.

The buzzer went for Assembly and they all ran off.

I picked myself up, aching all over, and cried a bit. I'd be in trouble but I wasn't going to let them see me like this. I washed my face and held my nose between my fingers till the bleeding slowed down.

Then I went to my classroom – passing through the hall where big notices said: **_This School has a No Bullying Policy_**. It was just words. Policies weren't much good – you'd got to find the thugs and punish them. But I wasn't going to be the one to tell on them.

The trouble was, my nose started bleeding again – and Josh was one of the first to see me clutching it in a bloody bit of bog roll when he came back to the classroom. 'Trouble again?' he asked.

'Yeah – but I'b nod telling,' I said indistinctly.

The others pretended not to see me and Snook the Snake came in then.

Of course she noticed straight away: 'Is your nose bleeding, Joanna?' she snapped, as if I'd done it on purpose.

I nodded, clutching it. I swear I could feel Sara's eyes boring into my back, willing me not to tell. 'I fell over, Miss,' I said. Someone – probably one of the Three Thugs – giggled.

Snook sent me to the sick room where kindly Mrs Love, nicknamed Lovey, the PE teacher who'd done First Aid, pinched the bridge of my nose with expert fingers and applied some ice. 'Your face is bruised a little,' she said as if she really minded.

'Fell over and banged into the locker,' I said.

'I think you'll live.' Lovey sent me back to the classroom when she was sure the bleeding had stopped.

Sneaky gave me a look but carried on with the lesson. I couldn't concentrate on the Maths test – all the time I was wondering how Sara had found out about Mum. It was the day before term started when Wendy took us all to see the school and Mum hadn't been back since. I reckoned she was scared of falling now and wouldn't try to get as far as the school.

PE was next. For a moment I was scared, going to the changing room, but Sara was sucking up to Sneaky by collecting all our papers. That's the sort of thing she always did. The teachers had no idea what she was really like.

Her Thugs, Angie and Jackie, were behind me and giggling together but they never did much without Sara. 'How's your poor little nose, Jo?' giggled bun-faced Angie.

My nose hurt but stood up to PE, which I'd always enjoyed. I was walking along the bar, pretending I was a famous gymnast, when Sara shrieked, 'There's a wasp on your hair, Jo!' I hate wasps so I swiped at my head, lost my balance and fell off. Sara and her friends led the giggles.

Lovey looked at them sharply but nobody could prove there hadn't been a wasp.

At the end of PE, Lovey stopped me, asking about my nose. By the time I reached the changing room, Sara was coming out, with her stupid friends. I put my hand inside the locker for my skirt and

41

shoes and my fingers went into something horribly soft and squidgy. Dear Sara's present to me was a bag of rotting vegetables – so rotten that it stank and was leaking out on my skirt.

I knew what happened if you told on someone and how could I prove Sara had done it? I threw the stinking mess away and did my best to wipe my skirt but there was a smelly damp patch on the back.

The next class was computer studies. I hurried to get to a computer and sit down but I heard Sara sniggering and Angie whispered, 'Wet herself like her brother!' Mr Clark, the teacher, was oldish and dozy and he didn't hear but some of the class did and there were more giggles. I found I was going red and trying not to cry but they were tears of rage! Today I hated Sara, the school and everything about my life.

When I collected Doddy, Mrs Meek said: 'I haven't heard from your mother yet. Have you a telephone at home, dear?'

'No,' I said truthfully. Wendy had the phone and I didn't know the number.

She sighed. 'I shall have to come and see her myself.'

'She's always out,' I said wildly. 'She sells cosmetics.'

She looked at me closely. 'I'm glad she's better

and back to work. But surely she's there for your tea?'

'No – I get the tea and mind Donald.' Then I thought Mum might get into trouble as I wasn't even thirteen.

'She's always back at night,' I added. Then I hurried Doddy away.

Mum sent me out for fish and chips when I got home – Wendy had actually paid her for some work. She said she was going upstairs to help her with some lists after supper.

This was my big chance to find Dad's address.

I left Doddy in front of the mini TV Wendy had lent us. She'd told us it was from her bedroom, just to make us feel grateful.

At first I felt guilty, searching Mum's bedroom, but I reminded myself that she'd no right to keep my dad's address secret. I found a small suitcase on top of the wardrobe and took it down. Of course it was locked. Where was the key?

'Jo?' said Doddy, from the doorway.

'You'll miss your programme,' I said. 'I'm just looking for something.'

'Doddy tell Mum.'

'If you do I won't go to the Zoo with you and you can't go on your own,' I said nastily. For once I was glad that he'd find it difficult to explain things to Mum. He started snuffling so I added: 'It'll be our secret, Dods.'

43

'Secret.' He grinned. 'OK – secret.' He trotted off again.

Sometimes Mum kept spare keys in what she called her trinket box, now on the chest of drawers. I looked inside and found several keys on a ring. One fitted the case.

My heart beat fast and guiltily as I rummaged amongst the papers – mostly boring things like our birth certificates and Post Office savings books. There was no address book. Right at the bottom was a large birthday card.

The outside was a painting of red roses and TO MY WONDERFUL WIFE and inside there was a lovey-dovey rhyme and Dad's writing: *To my darling beautiful wife Lizzie, with all my love for ever, your loving husband Alex and heaps of kisses.* This was a waste of time – no address. Then I saw the PTO and turned the card over.

PS. Am posting this from Loch Ness before we take off further north. I miss you a lot. Get better soon and I'm sorry about everything. I'll always remember what you did for me. Hope Doddy improves and tell Jo to go on practising those drums. I want to come to the Raving Rats' first garage gig when I get back. Here's a picture for the kids.

Tears came into my eyes as I saw one of his little drawings – of a bunch of bent, elderly holiday-makers and my large dad with a shepherd's crook, herding them on to the waiting coach. A Loch Ness

Monster was just behind them, snaking its head forward. It was brilliant! Mum had never even shown it to us.

PPS. Don't forget to write. I'll ring you from Sandy's when I get to London. Here's the bus company's address in case you've lost it and Sandy's if you want to write or ring. And he'd printed them both out, with phone numbers!

And I'd thought he must have forgotten her birthday, which was two days before we left. I reckoned the best thing was to write to both addresses, to make sure Dad got the letter. I copied them down, locked the case and put it and the key back where they belonged.

I'd hoped to write the letters and post them that evening but Doddy was in one of his whiney, difficult moods and wouldn't even watch TV. He kept on asking for Mum, who was still upstairs. In the end, I had to play a game he'd invented, when I was the cat and he was a rat, hiding from me with a great deal of squeaking.

Mum didn't come back until I'd persuaded Doddy to go to bed. 'She kept you for ages,' I complained exhaustedly.

'I'm sorry, darling,' she said. 'But we had coffee and a good chat. I need a bit of friendship at the moment.'

I could see what she meant but I wouldn't have chosen Wendy. I began to yawn and as soon as

45

Doddy was asleep, said I wanted to get to bed early. I had to write to Dad.

I found a page of Mum's typing paper and put the Grunge House address on top. Then I remembered I wanted to give him Wendy's telephone number. It was too late to ask Mum and she might have become suspicious. Also, I hadn't warned Mum that Doddy's teacher might visit her. I hoped Mrs Meek wouldn't come, or she'd find out I'd never delivered the letter. Well, by then Dad might be here and everything sorted out.

Our flat walls were thin and I could hear the printer churning out paper next door. Doddy was fast asleep, humped under his duvet with Rat. I decided to ask Mum once more why we couldn't go back.

I opened the living-room door quietly. Mum was just sitting, looking at the thin strip of town-pink night sky showing at the top of our window, above the dark dustbins and high wall.

'Mum,' I said.

She turned round and light from the computer screen shone on her wet cheeks. Then she tried to smile. 'I wish you were happier here, darling. It's not permanent, you know.' Did she mean we'd go back to Dad? But she said, 'Once I'm better I can get a proper job and our own place. And I am getting better with Wendy's help.'

'Dream on, Mum,' I wanted to say. She was just

the same and Doddy only a little bit better. But I only said, 'Why can't we go back to Dad? You've had a change. He needs us.'

She began to cry again. 'We can't, that's all. I can't explain at the moment. I'm sorry, darling . . .'

A year ago I'd have run and hugged her and cried too but I couldn't now she'd more or less told me she didn't want to go back – ever. I'd like to have asked her, too, why she hadn't shown us Dad's birthday card but I couldn't admit to looking through her private case.

Obviously it was up to me to get my parents together again. I took a deep breath. I didn't like lying to her but I had to. 'Doddy's teacher asked if we had a phone number. I didn't know it.'

Mum shuffled the papers that had come out of the printer. 'It's Wendy's number,' she said. 'It's not really for us to use.'

'If the teacher can't ring up she's going to come and see you.' I felt really mean and sneaky saying this but I had to get the number.

Mum sighed. 'I did explain about Doddy when he started there. But I'll write down the number for you to give her.'

'He'd be better back home,' I said hopefully. 'We both need to see Dad. Look at Doddy running away yesterday.'

'And I need space. Go to bed, Jo,' Mum said.

So I left her. At least I felt less guilty about going through her case. It was all her fault, leaving Dad.

I put the telephone number at the top, then wrote: *Dad – this is Wendy's number. Make her fetch me to the phone. I don't like it here and it's not helping Mum. Doddy's speaking more but not much. Mum needs you but she thinks she needs Wendy. Please come. I miss you mega-lots and the Raving Rats – I bet they get a new drummer if I don't get back soon. Heaps and heaps of love, Jo xxxxxxxx*

Most of the spelling looked OK to me. I then wrote the same letter to the coach company and put PERSONNALL AND URGENT on both letters like I'd seen Mum do on some of Wendy's envelopes.

Chapter 5

I woke up early next day, ready to post the letter but I needed stamps. Mum might have some. I found a book of stamps by the computer.

'Jo?' Doddy was standing in the doorway. I told him to go back to bed in case he woke Mum.

In fact, I was pouring out cereal for Doddy and me when she finally got up, looking very tired. She said she'd not slept very well. I reckoned it was all Wendy's fault, giving her so much work.

I didn't want Doddy to see me post the letters on the way to school in case he tried to tell Mum. There was a postbox just down the road. I told Mum I'd fetch the milk from the front step and rushed out – straight into Wendy, fetching her milk from the step. She was wearing a long purple night-dress and her black hair snaked over her shoulders.

'In a hurry, are you, Joanna?' she asked. 'Are those letters sticking out of your shirt?'

Nosy cow! 'So what?' I said rudely. 'I manage a pop group at home. We have to arrange gigs.' Well, we'd not quite got to that stage, though there was a chance of playing at another birthday party but Wendy wasn't to know that, was she? I tried to push past her and must have jogged her arm so she dropped a bottle. I heard her yelp as I ran down the road but I didn't dare stop until I'd posted the letters.

When I got back, Mum, balanced on one crutch, was trying to help her mop up milk flooding the hall. 'Really, Joanna!' she said. 'You could have stopped to help. And Wendy says you were off to the postbox.'

'She was in a hurry, like all the young people are, these days,' Wendy said, sighing in her irritating way.

I muttered that I was sorry and fetched another cloth. When we'd cleared up and had gone back to our flat, Mum asked me who I was writing to.

I hated telling porkies to her but I made it sound convincing. 'I've got to tell Mikey and the Group that we'll be back before winter or they'll get that Carl to be drummer instead of me.' Then I rushed off with Doddy before she could say anything.

I didn't take in anything at school. Would the coach company send on my letter to one of Dad's stopovers? Or would it just wait at the office and he'd get the one I sent to Sandy's on Friday night? Would he come straight away? Maybe the coach didn't get in till Saturday. Would he ring first? Then the awful thought came that he might have been so hurt by Mum taking us away that he'd not do anything at all, not even answer.

'Joanna – what are you doing?' Sneaky's voice cut into my thoughts.

We were supposed to be doing a comprehension test on a mind-blowingly boring description. Only Sneaky could rootle out the worst bit of a set book – when she'd been away ill, we'd had a different teacher who'd made the book seem quite interesting.

I found I'd drawn little pictures all round the text copy: a class of stick kids all slumped asleep on their desks with snores coming out in bubbles and Sneaky in front.

'I was thinking,' I said truthfully.

She'd made me sit in the front and now she swooped on my paper. 'You've written nothing in twenty minutes and you have completely messed up the paper with your childish drawings,' she hissed. 'But maybe Joanna can't understand the work,' she said to the class. 'We must be sorry for her and help her, mustn't we?'

I had to stand in front of the class while some of the others answered the questions out loud. Sneaky Snook ignored Josh because she knew he'd have some mega-clever explanation and asked the boy next to him, Alan. When he stood up to read, I saw he had a bandage on the forefinger of his right hand.

I hardly minded Sara and Co. sniggering at me as I stood – because my mind was whirling. Could

Alan be the boy I'd seen with the Eye? The boy I'd seen looked about twelve or so and St. Matthew's was the only Middle School in the town. He might very well be the boy who'd snatched the other Eye.

Josh had warned me against the Eyes but I was curious. I wanted to see through both of them like he had. And if I could see Alan – maybe if I wanted to I could see Dad. Perhaps in some way I could find out why Mum had left him.

How could I find out if Alan had the Eye? I tried to remember if I'd seen him at the fair. I'd ask Josh – if he was still talking to me.

I caught up with him at dinner-time. 'Was Alan at the fair?' I asked. 'I want to find out who's got the other Eye.'

'There were quite a few from school,' Josh said. 'Look – Jo.' He stopped in a doorway and we let the others stream past to the dining room. For a moment I was pleased. He didn't care if the other boys saw him with me and teased him. 'I'd leave that Eye alone or chuck it away, if I was you.'

'I want my dad back.' I wished I hadn't said it because it sounded pathetic and childish. 'My mum just went and left him.' Why should Josh care, anyway?

But he looked at me seriously through those round glasses. 'I'll tell you now – if you think about someone and look through both Eyes you can see the person and hear their thoughts in your head.

52

And if you just hold both Eyes, you get the thoughts on their own. First I tried Miss Snook.'

'And what happened?' This was really interesting!

'I saw her at home. She's got this ancient mother who can't remember anything and wanders around at night. And she's nasty to Miss Snook. Snook's dead scared she'll lose her job because she makes mistakes. And she's getting old.'

'She doesn't have to take it out on you.'

Josh smiled. 'It was really scary, getting her thoughts about me! She doesn't like me because I'm clever and she thinks I show her up. Then there were other people, some in the church; I only had to think about one of them when I had the Eyes and I was battered with thoughts; their hopes and fears – and their guilty secrets. For instance, there was a man, the church treasurer, who'd fiddled the accounts. I couldn't tell Dad what I knew because he'd not have believed me but a week later the man left the town suddenly and people found what he'd done.'

It all seemed so strange, like magic. But I'd long ago stopped believing in magic and yet . . . 'At least you didn't hear someone planning a murder,' I said, trying to speak in a jokey way because the whole thing was scary.

'You might find it funny. I didn't,' he snapped. 'I even tried just thinking of friendly people – like Lovey. I switched into her thoughts which were happy and OK but then she was worrying a lot about someone at school because she'd heard their parents got drunk and fought. Somehow I got into the boy's mind – well, I imagined it was a boy, and it was mega unhappy, filled with black murderous thoughts about his parents. He hated everyone and specially himself. It was horrible.'

'Did you get his name?'

'No – just vague, rambling thoughts about an unhappy home. I tried putting the Eyes away but somehow they kind of drew me like magnets. I *had* to look through them. I reckoned I was sort of addicted; the Eyes were a drug even though they made me upset – so I gave them to the church stall. But I reckon I should have binned them.'

'I think I've seen those quarrelling parents ...' I began and then a teacher told us to move on and I lost him in the crowd jostling into the dinner-hall.

Sara was queuing up for food behind Angie and Jackie. She turned and saw me. 'How's poor crippled mum and mental brother?' The dinner lady was ladling baked beans onto her plate. I gave Sara a great push. The worn-out plimsolls she always wore must have slipped and she fell into her plate of beans and chips. When she stood up, her face was red with juice and dripping beans and kids nearby laughed. The dinner lady looked angry and fetched a teacher.

The Thugs told on me of course, and I was sent

to sit in the corridor outside the Head's office until she was ready to see me. My being in trouble wouldn't do Mum any good – the Gorgon would certainly want to see her now. The buzzer went – people went rushing down the corridors and the teachers came out of their staff room opposite, leaving the door half open.

I saw their wall-phone just inside the room. Suddenly I wanted to talk to Dad so desperately that I did a really daft thing. I'd still got Sandy's and the bus company's telephone numbers and addresses in my pocket. Maybe the company would send him a message or even give me the number of his next night stop. It seemed too long to wait for my letters to arrive. Of course if I was like most of the other kids I'd have had my own mobile and used it on the way home but we'd never had much money to spare.

I walked to the door – peered round – nobody there – and tore inside. I'd got my dinner-money. I punched out the number of the bus company first and put in ten pence. All the time I was watching through the crack in the door in case someone came.

'Highland Tours,' said a voice.

'Could I leave a message for a driver, Alexander Murray?' I asked.

'Is it urgent? He's away in Scotland with the coach.'

'Please – it's urgent. Tell him his daughter rang and he must come.'

My money ran out just as Lovey appeared. 'What are you doing, Joanna?' she asked but with a friendly smile. 'The staff room is out of bounds, as you know.'

I couldn't lie to her. 'I've been trying to ring my dad,' I said.

'Is something wrong?' That was just like her, instead of lecturing me about using the staff room phone.

'No – yes!' and to my horror I burst into tears. 'And I've got to see the Gorgon – I mean, the Head.'

'Come on, dear.' She led me to the Gorgon's door and knocked.

I heard the familiar bark. 'Come in.'

'Joanna was just explaining to me why she was waiting for you,' Lovey said smoothly. 'I think something is upsetting her at home.'

'Joanna has just upset our dinner queue,' the Gorgon said severely, glancing at a note on her desk. 'She attacked Sara Woods. Did Sara push you first, Joanna?'

I shook my head.

Lovey touched my arm, lightly, as if she wanted to remind me of something. Then she said she had to go.

When she opened the Head's door, Josh was

waiting outside. He walked in without being asked. 'I heard what Sara Woods said before Jo pushed her,' he said calmly. 'She called Jo's mum a cripple and her brother mental. My dad's always going on about turning the other cheek but I'd have slapped Sara's if she'd said that to me.'

The Gorgon thanked him for coming to see her and sent him back to the class. 'Sit down, Joanna,' she said and actually smiled at me! 'Sara was very unkind to say what she did but you must learn some self-control. Sometimes it's better to ignore hurtful remarks. But is it partly true? You said your mother was better?'

I looked at her big, squarish hands. 'OK. It's true. Mum's still not well and Doddy – well he isn't the same as before the accident. He doesn't talk properly.'

'Can you tell me just what happened?'

I had to force myself to answer. 'Mum, Dad and Doddy were coming to collect me from the form disco. I'd just started at the Comprehensive. We're right in the country – the school's about eight miles away.' I stopped.

Confused images jumbled round my brain. I could still remember it so clearly, too clearly. The disco music and lights; me dancing in a sort of muddle with my mates from the group. Mikey was just yelling something about giving them live music from the Raving Rats next year – and I was yelling back something like, 'Dream on!' when the music stopped suddenly and there was the voice of Big Sir – Mr Williams, the Head – speaking through the mike, asking for me.

That was the end of my old life and the beginning of this crappy new one. Me – seeing Mum and Doddy in hospital and my bouncy, smiley dad totally changed. I was completely gutted to find him crying, several times.

Doddy was out of hospital quite quickly but he wouldn't speak. They kept Mum in for several weeks because she had to have operations on her leg. When she came home, she'd changed too – worrying all the time about Doddy and snappy with Dad – when it was all her fault anyway as she was driving. I heard them quarrelling when I was in bed.

All this flashed through my head quickly as I wondered how much to tell the Gorgon. 'Mum was driving,' I said reluctantly. 'She didn't usually but they'd been celebrating Dad's new job. She doesn't drink but he does a bit. Not a lot,' I said quickly. 'It was dark down the country road. I suppose she was going too fast and she drove into the back of a van. The front of our car sort of crumpled. Somehow all Dad got was a cut on his head but her legs got caught. My brother must've undone his straps because he shot forward and banged his head.' Why was I saying all this? But the Gorgon was listening; did I imagine it or were her beady eyes softer?

'I'm really sorry, Joanna.' Then she paused. She looked at a file in front of her. 'Your mother gave me the impression you would be here for some time, living with her friend. I understood your parents were almost permanently separated.'

I looked at her. Then I remembered Mum asking me to wait in Wendy's car while they both talked to the Head. I'd been so gutted at having to go to this crappy school instead of my own that I'd not cared what they said. I'd just sat in the car, hating everyone. 'She told me it was just while she was getting better.'

'I'm sorry. I thought you knew . . .' The Gorgon looked uncomfortable. 'I need to talk to your mother about next term.'

'We'll be going home,' I said. 'Dad's coming . . .' I began, then I stopped. I didn't know that he would come, did I? My stomach churned and I felt like throwing up at the thought of staying at Grunge House for ever.

The Gorgon cleared her throat. 'I hope it all works out for the best, Joanna.' She obviously wasn't going to take sides. 'But you could help yourself to be happier here if you tried harder in all ways. It's Miss Snook's last term – she's retiring, owing to personal problems. I think you'll find if you co-operate with her, she'll get on better with you.' She smiled. 'Now I need to talk to Sara. Apart from saying nasty things today – has she been bullying you at all?'

I crossed my fingers behind my back and shook my head.

The Gorgon cleared her throat. 'Because this school doesn't tolerate bullies. Remember, though, that Sara herself may have problems of her own at home. Don't ever forget that people are like icebergs.' She fixed me with her old Gorgon-like stare.

'Icebergs?' I asked, wondering if she'd gone off her trolley.

'Two-thirds of them are submerged – we don't know all the things other people have to put up with which may make them angry and difficult.'

The next class was my favourite, Art. It was a relief to get away from Sneaky Snook and the teacher liked my pictures. Today we could do what we wanted. The teacher was putting pictures on the wall for Parents' Evening. I was painting a picture of the Raving Rats at a gig when I saw Sara coming in late. Her face was angry.

As she came past my table she stumbled and jogged it so my paint-water flooded down over the painting. 'Oh, sorry,' she said loudly. 'You'd got it balanced right on the edge!' Angie and Jackie giggled. The paper was cockling up – the picture spoilt. I forgot the Gorgon's talk and jabbed a brush full of red paint at Sara's face.

Of course there was trouble again. Sara said she'd not done anything and nobody else dared speak. Josh, who was sitting next to me, had been fetching paint-water, so he'd not seen anything either.

My soggy painting wasn't proof – Sara said she just jogged the table by accident. The teacher said our behaviour belonged to the infant school and made us sit in front of the class as models for them to draw. There was a lot of giggling and whispered nasty remarks about our funny faces or big feet.

'You told on me,' Sara hissed.

I didn't answer, though I was boiling inside. It was only then I noticed the plaster on the finger of her right hand.

Chapter 6

When Doddy was asleep that night, I got the Eye down from its shelf. It shone by the light of my bedside lamp. Maybe I could see Dad if I thought about him hard but as I looked through the black centre it melted into a dimly-lit living room. The light from a TV gleamed on the other Eye, which lay on the floor. In front of it, the boy was huddled on a cushion, asleep. The crack and the usual mist made everything indistinct. The overhead light flicked on and I saw how tatty the room was. There were empty glasses, bottles and plastic takeaway dishes all over the floor. The big woman came into my view and the sleeper was hauled up roughly. I could tell by her expression she was shouting at him again. She must have seen the Eye, for she bent to pick it up but the boy was too quick and snatched it first, running to the door.

Doddy called out indistinctly. I put down the Eye and pulled the duvet snugly round him, making soothing noises.

When he'd settled, I looked into the Eye again. This time I saw into the bedroom. The other Eye was in the boy's hand. There was something dark against the door. Then he ran to the window and

62

my Eye followed him bumpily, like a hand-held video camera. I saw him hanging by the ledge for a moment, then dropping to a flat roof and jumping to the ground. My Eye tracked him, down a misty road lit by street lights and then running into a moonlit park. I recognised the bandstand, the dark shape of the church; it was our park!

The chestnut blossom glimmered palely on the big trees and the moonlight glinted on the slides and swings. The boy sat on a swing and swung up and down.

I suddenly thought that if I hurried out there, I could find out for sure who had the other Eye. If I could get hold of it I could use both Eyes to see Dad and hear his thoughts as well.

I put on my track suit and crept across the room to the door, carrying the Eye. Doddy stirred and said, 'Jo . . . Jo . . .' I waited. No good if he gave the alarm – it would just worry Mum and achieve nothing.

He went back to sleep and I opened the door carefully, slipped through and was out of our front door and into the hall. I tiptoed to the front door, opening it as quietly as I could. I ran all the way down the street and across the park to the play-ground. It was empty but the swing was going up and down as if someone had just left. I sat on it, disappointed. Then I looked down and saw the moonlight shining on something at my feet. I jumped off the swing and picked up – the other Eye!

I ran home as fast as I could with both Eyes in my pocket.

When I came to Grunge House I remembered I'd rushed out without my key. If I rang the bell, would I get Mum or Wendy? I ran down the basement stairs. There was an old cellar door – locked. The bedrooms had bars over the windows, like a prison. I walked round the house and saw our living-room window was shut tight.

I ran back to the front door. I'd have to ring the bell. I held the Eyes in my pocket with my free hand as a kind of insurance.

The door opened and it was Wendy, wrapped in her dark dressing-gown. Her face without the Magic Make-up was dead pale and her eyes glittered in the street light.

'Come in at once, Joanna!' she whispered. 'Where have you been at this time of night?' *How can I deal with this child? Her behaviour isn't doing poor Lizzie any good.* The words darted into my brain but Wendy hadn't spoken yet. The Eyes were seeing her thoughts.

As I came inside I kept hearing her thoughts: *I so want to help Lizzie and her family but the children have been disturbed by moving . . . It's made Joanna totally out of hand. I imagine she wants her father, it's only natural. It might be better if she knew her mother wants to leave him for good after that acci-dent. I don't know how to advise her . . .*

The thoughts bombarded me in the space of a heartbeat as we came into the hall. She'd got the wrong end of the stick.

'She mustn't leave him – he's done nothing wrong!' I burst out.

Wendy backed away from me, looking almost scared. 'How did you know . . .' she began.

Mum must've heard the noise because she shot out of our front door, white like she'd seen a ghost.

The rest doesn't bear telling; Wendy told Mum I might have been murdered, out on my own at night. Mum said it was past midnight but she didn't ask me where I'd been until we were back in our flat.

How could I explain? I said I'd been sort of sleep-walking. She'd never have believed my story about the Eyes. Mum didn't answer. Then the talking in my head started again. *It's all my fault for coming here. Not fair to upset Joanna's life. Just couldn't bear Alex being so full of self-pity and guilt. And Wendy's just not used to children . . . she's so lonely and she's afraid I'll go back to Alex.*

This time I remembered not to answer her thoughts but the sadness in her made me want to cry although I didn't understand it all. 'I'm sorry,' I said.

I felt worse because Mum was nice to me and made me hot chocolate. All she said was that the

65

streets weren't safe at night at my age and we'd talk in the morning.

I waited until Doddy went back to sleep and then put on my pencil torch. I put each Eye against mine and thought of Dad. Nothing happened. I just saw the faint gleam of the torchlight through them.

I went on staring but I wondered if it was any good trying to see him. Even if he got my letter and came to Grunge House, Mum didn't want to go back to him. I felt angry – I know she and Doddy had suffered from the accident but wasn't it quite natural that my dad would be upset? Perhaps he went on at her when I wasn't there, about it being her fault? Getting them together seemed almost impossible so maybe that was why the Eyes didn't let me see him.

I tried not to think of my dad. I still hadn't solved the puzzle of who had had the other Eye.

Suddenly I could see clearly with both Eyes, much better than with one. The crack hardly bothered me. There was a room lit by a thin shaft of moonlight through a gap in the curtains, a bigger room than before. There were two beds and dark shapes of cases and bags on the floor. I tried to see who lay in the beds but all I could make out was two humps of bedclothes. Sadness leaked out of the room and confused, black thoughts: *It was more her fault than Dad's, all that fighting, so why leave him? I hate them both. . .*

The thoughts filled my head, pushing mine away so I felt taken over by another mind. I just couldn't bear it. I put both Eyes in the pocket of my school jacket and turned off the torch.

Chapter 7

Luckily we all overslept, so Mum didn't get a chance to ask me anything and Doddy didn't remember to ask for his Eye. As I came through the park to school I saw someone in the playground, wandering round, bending down now and again as if searching for something. I dragged Doddy over there and saw – Sara!

'No! Yuk! Nasty girl!' Doddy whimpered but I took no notice.

'Looking for something?' I asked.

'Get lost!' she said. Her face was all puffy and her eyes red.

My hand in my pocket, I held the Eyes as if she could snatch them from me. Thoughts battered at my brain: *Where is it? It's all I got left ... and someone's taken it. Thought it would bring me luck – dream on, Sara. I hate living with Mum in this place and there's this uppity new girl looking down her nose like Lady Muck. She needs showing I'm someone at school – that's the only place I'm in control ... Bet she's got it ...*

The thoughts came so fast and so bitter I took a step back. No wonder Josh couldn't bear it; my brain felt scrambled with her thoughts mixed with mine. So it was *Sara* I'd seen! I'd try to help her. The other Eye was no help to me to get Dad back and I didn't want to go off my trolley, ghetto-blasted with sad, angry thoughts. I'd try to forget her bullying and help her. I felt good as I held the Eye out. 'Is this what you lost? Found it last night.'

'Gimme!' she yelled, grabbing it. 'Following me, were you?'

I stared. She should have been grateful. 'I got the other Eye; I saw you coming out here.' I couldn't hear her thoughts now so I didn't know why she was still mad at me.

'Fancy your mum letting little Jo Jo out at night!' she sneered. Then her voice changed, became uncertain. 'It's scary, this magic Eye thing. I seen you but kind of fuzzy only I guessed it's you because of your mum with crutches. I suppose you've seen me.' She grabbed my arm. 'You dare tell that my parents drink and fight. I'm with my mum now but I hate her.'

I didn't know what to say. I couldn't imagine hating either of my parents even if I did blame Mum for moving and for the accident. I looked at my watch. 'Come on, we're late!' I said.

Sneaky Snook bit our heads off. I tried hard to think of her ancient mum and how tired she must be but I still didn't like her. I saw Josh looking at us and I was sure if I had both Eyes I'd have known he was wondering why Sara and I had come in late together.

We got into more trouble later on. Sneaky was writing something on the board when I was passed a note. Everyone was giggling as they'd read it on the way: *Let's have your eye then I'll know what the stupid old bat is thinking. S.* Of course nobody knew what Sara meant. Sneaky turned round as I was reading the note and the others were giggling obediently – they often laughed at any joke the Three Thugs made to save trouble for themselves.

Sneaky pounced on the note. 'I recognise this writing – Sara, stand up.'

Sara lolled, smiling insolently, but I forced myself to feel sorry for her and put up my hand. 'She just wants to borrow something of mine, Miss.'

'Three eyes are better than one!' someone said, giggling.

'Give her your eye, Jo, or she'll tear it out!' That was Alan. Of course, everyone (except Josh, who looked bored) joined in with sillier and sillier remarks until Sneaky banged her desk and ordered Sara and me to spend the rest of the lesson sitting outside the Head's office.

'You ought to thank me – it's better here than listening to old Sneaky boring on,' Sara said.

'Did you really think I'd pass the Eye to you?'

She took a bag of toffees from her pocket. 'Have one.' I could hardly believe this was Sara! Then she said, 'Go on – let me have yours. I want to hear what the Head thinks. Go on – I need a bit of fun after all that's happened.'

I looked at her shadowed eyes and felt sorry for her. 'OK – just while we're here.' I gave her my Eye and she thrust her hand in her skirt pocket.

'I'll hold them both,' she said.

Morgan the Gorgon came out of her office. 'Ah – you again?' she said, rather sadly. 'Tell me what happened.'

'Nothing much,' Sara said. 'We were just too noisy, I suppose.' She looked down meekly.

'See that neither of you is sent out of class again this term,' the Gorgon said. She was obviously going to say more only her telephone was ringing and she went to answer it.

Sara waited until the door shut. 'It works,' she said. 'But it's weird. I don't know if I like it. She's sorry for us both. Something about *those poor girls and their difficult backgrounds. Perhaps they will make friends and help each other now.* Friends! Patronising old git!' Sara added but feebly, as if she didn't altogether mean it.

'Give it back now, please,' I said.

'Wait a sec – want to hear what someone else is thinking.'

The buzzer went and the Two Thugs came out of the classroom in front of everyone else. 'Come on, Sara – fancy having to sit with *her*,' Angie said.

'That Josh's been showing off as usual,' said Jackie. 'I just bumped into him accidentally on purpose and his books went all over the floor!' She giggled. 'How's the mental brother and the crippled mum, Jo?'

I was so angry that I could've killed her but I kept quiet. In my head, I imagined jumping up and down on them till they screamed for mercy.

'Look out – Jo wants to kill you both!' Sara said. 'And her brother's not mental – he's been in an accident.'

Angie looked at her as if she'd gone ape. 'Mini little Jo hurt *us*! Pull the other one, Sara! You on her side or something?'

'Let's leave Sara – she's got ickle Jo Jo now for her best friend!' Shrieking with laughter, Angie and Jackie walked away.

'Wait for me – you're my gang!' Sara ran after them and the milling crowd of kids changing classes swallowed them up.

'Sara – give my Eye back!' I shouted after her. People looked at me curiously as I followed them and then Josh was beside me in the corridor. 'What's up?' he asked.

'Sara's got both the Eyes!' I had to shout above the noise of the crowd.

'Let her!' he yelled back. 'I bet she'll give them both back by the end of the day. It's awful, hearing other people's thoughts buzzing in your brain. Wait and see – it'll teach her a lesson!'

I wasn't sure he was right. It'd give her power and Sara needed power to get back her position as leader of the Three Thugs. Somehow, I wanted to get her on my side, so I could have Doddy's Eye back and borrow hers too. If I could hear Mum's thoughts, I might understand why she'd left Dad – and then when he came to see me, after my letter got to him, I'd somehow get them together.

I tried asking her at dinner-time but she looked weird and ran off without finishing her chips. I ran after her to the loos – but she'd locked herself in. I hung around with the kids who were hiding there to smoke or just natter – then the buzzer went and I had to go to the classroom.

When school finished, I waited by the gate. Most of my form streamed past but not Sara. Then I saw her, with the Two Thugs. I ran after them, pushing past people and caught up just as they were going out of the gates. 'Sara!' I yelled. She looked round, telling me to get lost.

I stopped feeling sorry for her, ran up and grabbed at the plastic bag she always took to school. It tore and everything spilled out.

I saw the Eyes, glittering in the afternoon sunshine, and dived for them but Angie swung her heavy school bag and hit me hard on the head, knocking me to the ground so my breath seemed to be forced out of my body and my head reeled. I struggled up, my head splitting and dimly saw Sara picking everything up. My arms were grabbed and the Thugs marched me out of the school gates, linking arms in mine, making it look as if we were great mates. I dimly heard Sara behind us, telling the Thugs to let me go.

They frog-marched me down to the park and into the loos there. I guessed what was coming but they were bigger than me and I couldn't move. Sara was behind them. I thought she called out, 'Let her go!' but the Thugs were out of her control now. I tried yelling but they bent me over and pushed my face into the smelly loo and water roared down as they pulled the chain. Then they were gone and I staggered to my feet, soaked. I threw up – then washed my face in the basin outside. There was a smeary mirror there with rude messages scrawled on it in lipstick. I was a real mess, my forehead bruised and my wet hair clinging to my head.

I looked at my watch and ran out into the sunshine. It was four o'clock. At Doddy's school, they always kept him till I came at three-thirty. I'd never been so late before!

My legs felt like wobbly jelly and the sunshine seemed to hurt my eyes as I tried to run.

All the mums' and dads' cars had gone and there

was a padlock on the security fence. Didn't the head teacher stay on for a bit? Obviously not today.

Someone must have taken Doddy home. I was in big trouble.

Chapter 8

I heard the voices as I let myself in the front door.

'Where have you *been*?' Mum pounced on me as soon as I got inside our flat. Doddy's teacher was there in our living room and Wendy hovered threateningly over Mum, who was clutching a crying Doddy.

'It shouldn't be too much for you to come back with your brother!' Mum said. Then she looked at me and gave a kind of yelp. 'What have you been doing? There's a huge bruise on your forehead and you're all wet!'

'I'm sorry about Dods,' I said. I wasn't going to be one of those kids who sneaked. Plus, if I did, the Thugs would find some way to punish me when nobody was looking. 'I fell down heaps of stone steps at school. Someone splashed water on me to revive me.' That sounded quite good.

'Why didn't they ring here?' Mum asked.

'Couldn't get through – maybe the phone's got a fault or something.'

Mrs Meek smiled at me. 'Poor Joanna! At any rate, I've had a chance for a few words with you, Mrs Murray – and with your friend. It's really a bit of a responsibility for Joanna, picking up Donald and it's not always convenient for staff to wait with him for half an hour. Could you make other arrangements? I can see Mrs Murray has difficulty walking ... could you manage to pick him up, Mrs Jolly?'

Though I was feeling grotty, I wanted to giggle. I'd forgotten Wendy's name was Jolly; she should be called Mrs Saddo!

Mum sent me off to wash and change but I heard Wendy saying of course she'd help sometimes, but she was so busy, that she couldn't possibly manage every day ...

I washed the loo-smell out of my hair and face and took off my clothes. Then I suddenly felt mega-heavy, weighed down with sleep. I lay on my bed.

'Jo!' Mum was there. 'Are you feeling all right?'

I struggled up through clouds of sleep. My head felt strange – as if someone really fat was sitting on it. 'Have they gone?' I asked but the words came out thick and slow.

Mum said they had and Wendy would pick Doddy up next day. 'Mrs Meek is worried about him,' she was saying when Doddy came in carrying a cup of Ribena and a nibbled chocolate biscuit.

'For you,' he said. 'Make better.'

I nearly cried but I decided to pretend I felt fine. Mum mustn't be worried now, with my dad probably ringing or arriving soon. I used a bit of

Positive Thinking to push down my fears that he wouldn't come.

I let Mum fuss over me a bit, because it was cosy to sit in front of the telly with a mug of hot chocolate. I couldn't eat anything but the chocolate took the taste of the bog-water away.

I did tell her my head ached so she gave me a couple of painkillers. 'Wendy wouldn't approve!' She tried to smile.

'No – she'd say headaches don't really exist, like ghosts! Just keep on with the Positive Thinking.' I giggled, though it made my head worse and I was pleased when Mum joined in.

I went to bed early and dreamed I was running away from the Thugs. But my legs wouldn't work and they pounced on me, sitting on my head so I couldn't breathe . . . I woke up calling out, 'Don't! Don't!'

Mum was there telling me I was dreaming. She felt my forehead and said I was hot. Then of course Dods got out of bed. 'Poor Jo,' he said, looking at me. He fetched Rat and tucked him under my bedclothes, I kissed my little brother and tried to sleep, tossing and turning the rest of the night.

The next day I felt so tired I just slept on and off most of the time. Mum kept coming in, feeling my forehead and trying to give me something to eat. My head ached and I felt a bit sick; all I wanted was to be left alone. My thoughts seemed to slide round my head, confused and scary, mixed with nightmares or were they daymares? – when Sara and the Thugs ran after me and then I was being sucked into a giant Eye and I knew I'd disappear like those stars into a black hole ...

I woke, and heard Mum saying she wanted to take me to the doctor but I pleaded with her to let me sleep and I knew I'd be better tomorrow. I had to be better because Dad might come ...

I got out of bed in the morning and the room spun round. I fell down. Doddy yelled and Mum came hobbling. She said she'd need to take me to the doctor. I argued I was OK – I had to show the Thugs I wasn't scared of them and I wanted to get the Eye back but Mum went upstairs to use Wendy's telephone for an appointment.

She came back saying Wendy had offered to take Doddy to school and she'd ordered a taxi for Mum and me, saying she'd pay. The words were somehow muffled but I vaguely thought Wendy was kind.

We left Wendy trying to calm Doddy, who was in tears. 'It's more about his prize trip to the Zoo than anything,' Mum said. 'Wendy's got an all day Magic Make-up Conference on Saturday and she said she couldn't take you. I promised Donald a ride on a bus with you but now he can see you're ill.'

'Better in a tick,' I said thickly, sounding kind of

drunk. Then I dozed off until Mum woke me at the doctor's.

After Dr Jenkins had examined me, she said I needed to go to the hospital for a scan to see if there was any hidden damage to my skull.

This meant another taxi and then a long wait when I kept on dozing off and then feeling sick. Mum tried to cheer me up but I knew she was worried. At last I had the scan, which was a bit scary but the nurses were jokey and kind. Then more waiting until another doctor came to talk to us.

The really gross thing was that he said I'd to stay in hospital the rest of the day and that night 'for observation'. I wanted to go home with Mum – because today was Friday; Dad might be back early from the coach trip and ring us up. I imagined Wendy somehow putting him off.

I was too tired to argue. Mum bought me a tooth-brush and a big tee shirt from the hospital shop to wear in bed. 'Well, it's me leaving you in hospital this time!' she said, trying to laugh. 'Only till tomorrow.'

'Early?' I asked.

'I'll ring them first thing.'

Fancy being in a children's ward at my age! The kids ranged from toddlers upwards. It was a bit like the ward Doddy was in after the accident, toys all over the place, nurses who didn't wear uniform and noise . . . noise! Mums and dads were in and out all the time and the nurse said some stayed at the hospital. I wished Mum had stayed. I wished everyone would shut up and let me sleep.

I'd seen a doctor – who was OK but talked to me as if I was about six. Then I was lying there closing my eyes against the bright lights when a nurse said: 'Joanna – a visitor for you.'

Why did I think it could be Dad? Sara was there – dead white and staring at me. 'Your mum said you were here for the night,' she said. 'I got the bus.' She threw a jumbo Twickers bar on the bed. 'Bet the food's gross,' she said.

I was dead surprised and kind of pleased. After all, she had tried to stop the Thugs. 'Thanks.'

'Did you tell your mum what they did to you?'

So that's why she'd come! She was scared there'd be trouble even though she'd not hit me herself. 'No.' I turned my head away.

'I've dumped them – Angie and Jackie,' she said. 'They didn't ought to have done it. 'Sides I'm sick of them anyway.'

'Get real, Sara! They dumped *you* after the park, I bet.'

'Yeah – we had a row.' I dimly saw a bruise on her face. 'I reckon that Josh guessed Angie and Jackie duffed you up. The Twickers is from both of us. He followed me round to your mum's after school. Seemed worried.' She paused. 'I've brought them.' She dumped a Tesco bag on the bed. 'Don't want them Eyes. Couldn't get my head together with all that talk and I got muddled because it wasn't so easy to hate. I've heard Mum's thoughts and Dad's and they're unhappy too and sorry. They want to get together again.'

'So it'll be better?' Why was I caring about Sara, of all people?

'Sort of. I reckon when they get together the drinking will start again and then the shouting. Folk don't change that quick.'

As she slouched out of the ward, I thought she seemed thirteen, going on thirty.

She'd knotted up the bag as if the Eyes might escape. My fingers were all fumbly as I undid it. I held the Eyes in my hand. *I'm scared. I want my mum!* I heard from the next bed. The boy with the bandage round his head was calmly reading a comic as if he wasn't scared at all.

More thoughts came – grown-up thoughts from nurses about boyfriends and tiredness and fears for some kids and then weird thoughts from the little kids and all sorts from the big children. It was awesome: like being attacked by radio stations from all over the world at once. Some of their worries and fears filled me and my head began to ache again.

I put the Eyes back in the bag with the Twickers bar – shoving them onto the table by my bed. At least they were there to help me tomorrow ... tomorrow when Dad might come.

Then I asked for paper from the hospital Play Leader and drew a funny picture of the boy in the next bed completely wrapped in bandages, waving his arms and stick-figures of nurses and doctors running away. I wrote at the bottom, 'Here is you as the ghost of a Mumy!' and sneaked over to his bed to give it to him. He actually laughed.

I didn't sleep well because kids cried and nurses trotted about and they kept waking me up to do something called checking my blood pressure, as if I might explode at any time.

Being in a hospital made me think about the accident.

Why did Mum hit that van? She'd never drink and drive, and when Dad was out of work she drove herself miles to work and back each day, no problem at all. My head felt jumbled. Perhaps they'd been quarrelling and she wasn't concentrating properly.

I tossed about and when I did sleep, I dreamed I was driving the car with Mum, Dad and Doddy in the seat behind. Suddenly an immensely tall Wendy ran out into the road and waved her arms in the headlights and at the same time the Thugs reached out from the back seat and gripped me round the neck.

The nurse said I'd got a good pair of lungs, from the screaming I'd done!

I felt much better the next day but the nurse said I couldn't go home until the doctor had seen me. When I was sure nobody was looking I held the Eyes and tried to concentrate on Dad through all the thoughts of the ward. At last I saw him telephoning in a dark little hall. He was talking – but I couldn't hear because a kid was yelling. I felt the cold sadness of his thoughts and then a nurse came to take my temperature and blood pressure and I had to put the Eyes away. Perhaps Dad had rung us and Wendy had put him off. I felt sad and suddenly so tired that I went to sleep again.

At last the doctor came round and said I could go home after lunch but I had to take it easy for a few days.

I couldn't eat. I kept on thinking about Dad – what would he do now? Would he just give up? I must have been crying because a nurse came along and asked me if I had another headache. I said I was fine – supposing they kept me in even longer?

I was dressed and ready for Mum long before she came.

What was she doing? I'd got my watch on now and saw it was nearly three. What had happened? At last, though, Mum hobbled into the ward, crutches gone and leaning on a stick!

'I've just had a chat with Sister and she says you're just to be quiet for a few days,' she said, giving me a forced sort of smile.

'How come, no crutches?' I asked.

'They said I could try to do without them – weeks back. I just didn't feel I could manage.'

My legs were wobbly so we sort of leaned on each other across the ward. 'What happened – why were you so late?' I asked.

'It was Doddy. Wendy had a terrible time with him yesterday. She had to carry him into the car. She wasn't best pleased as you can imagine. He refused to come here with me in the taxi today so I just had to leave him with her. She's got to go to her Conference soon so we must hurry.'

'Were there any phone calls for us?' I asked as we went down in the lift.

'No – why? I rang the school and said where you were. By the way, they didn't seem to know about you falling down those stone steps.'

'You probably got the wrong teacher.' Why was I bothering to protect the Two Thugs?

All the way home in the taxi, I felt something was wrong. Not just Doddy driving Wendy up the wall but something worse. When Mum was looking out of the window I felt in the Tesco bag and held the Eyes. I'd like to have looked through them but Mum would have thought I was going mad.

I got the taxi driver's thoughts: mainly about money he owed and his indigestion – then Mum's about Doddy – then what felt like alarm calls from Wendy. What had happened?

We arrived and there she was on the doorstep, dead white and her face like someone had died. As we got out she called: 'I couldn't stop him! Doddy's gone!'

Chapter 9

'Gone? What do you mean?' Mum was clutching my arm so hard it hurt.

'You must be brave, Lizzie,' Wendy said. 'Come on in. All things work for good in the end.'

I was still holding the Eyes and Wendy's thoughts came: *She'll see what Alex is really like, taking the boy away . . . She has to stay here to get well . . .*

'So my dad's been here!' I shouted.

'How did you know?' I tuned in to her and she was thinking: *Now I've upset my poor Lizzie and she was getting a little better . . . what shall I do?*

'I just did.'

'What are you talking about?' Mum asked as Wendy and I helped her up the steps and into the hall.

Wendy hugged her. 'Yes, Lizzie. Alexander came here, demanding to see you. He'd rung earlier. Donald rushed out and hung onto his father – muttering something I couldn't hear. Before I could say anything, Alexander had taken him off.'

Mum clung to Wendy. 'Could he have taken him to Sandy's house in London?' she asked. 'Sandy's wife's got children of her own and Doddy likes her.

Alexander couldn't look after him with all the coach driving to do.'

'Maybe they've just gone for a walk,' Wendy said but obviously she didn't believe it.

I held the Eyes and willed them to show me Doddy and Dad. Where were they?

Happiness flooded my mind and I heard Doddy laughing. I put the Eyes against mine and I could see them now, getting off a bus, and walking to a turnstile. I followed them through as Dad showed Doddy's free tickets and saw the big enclosures, the elephants ahead – a sign pointing TO THE GIRAFFES and Dad having to run to keep up with Doddy as he charged along happily.

'What are you doing with those silly glass things?' Mum asked. 'We ought to be out looking for them.' She looked really upset.

'Don't worry. I know where they are,' I said. Today was Saturday; the day of Doddy's prize treat.

The doorbell rang and I found Josh and Sara standing there.

I knew Wendy was behind me so I used the last of my strength and almost fell down the steps, clutching at my friends. 'Quick – or they'll stop me!'

'You OK now?' Josh asked.

'Of course she's not, you prat!' Sara lugged me along the street at a great rate – I was glad of it as my legs felt wobbly. Josh ran beside us. I thought I heard Wendy and Mum call out. I had some idea that they might drive after us and bring me back. 'I've got to go to the Zoo to find my brother!' I gasped.

'There's a bus from the Square,' Josh said.

'What about money?' Sara asked. 'I'm skint.'

'Me too,' I said.

'It's OK. I can pay,' Josh said. 'Paper-round plus pocket money.'

All the time we were getting to the bus stop I expected Wendy to turn up but nothing happened. Of course we had to wait for what seemed like ages while I worried about Mum. I wished now I'd said I knew Doddy was at the Zoo. But would she have believed me?

Once we were on the bus, I had to put the Eyes back in the plastic bag because I was dizzy with faint, tearful thoughts from Mum, happy feelings from Doddy and Dad at the Zoo, noises of animals, all mixed up with the thoughts of people on the bus.

Josh saw me. 'You still got them both,' he said. 'Wonder you aren't completely round the twist by now.'

The entrance tickets at the Zoo took all the rest of Josh's money – I saw him empty his pockets.

There were quite a lot of people about and I'd have to use the Eyes to find Doddy and Dad. I held them but again I couldn't bear it. I had thoughts from everyone, so confused and melting into each other that I couldn't really understand anything. Strongest of all I got a very bored feeling from the elephants in the enclosure just ahead, and wistful picture-thoughts of them walking in a big jungle and eating leaves off trees.

'It's the Eyes,' Josh said. 'Try thinking about your brother.'

I concentrated on Doddy and saw him on a bridge with Dad, looking down at some tigers in a grassy enclosure. 'They're at the tigers' cage!' I shouted and we ran, following the signs.

When we got there, they were still there, Dad holding Doddy up so he could see the tigers. I waved and called. People turned round as Dad saw me and charged through them, towing Doddy behind him. He hugged me, almost driving the breath out of my body. 'Jo! I was coming back to see you and Mum. Then Wendy said she didn't know when you'd be back. Doddy told me about his prize so I thought we'd go to the Zoo.'

I'd forgotten how large and comforting he was. 'Mum wants you,' I said. 'We all need you.'

Doddy was half laughing, half crying. 'Why've you come, Jo?' Then he noticed me holding the Eyes. 'Give me the Eye!' he shouted, spacing out his words but still talking more like a five-year-old.

'He sounds more like he used to!' I was so

pleased. Maybe seeing Dad had given his speech a kind of jolt.

'Yes, but what's he talking about?' Dad asked.

In the excitement I'd almost forgotten Josh and Sara. Now Josh said, quietly, 'You chuck the Eyes away somewhere, Jo. They tell you too much.'

'Yeah. You can't deal with it,' Sara agreed.

I knew they were right. 'Where can we hide them? Someone could get hold of them and make money out of them, couldn't they?'

'What are you on about?' Dad asked.

'Give them to me,' Josh said. I did. He ran back to the bridge and threw the Eyes down into the tigers' enclosure. A tiger ambled slowly forward, tail waving from side to side. He sniffed at the Eyes. Then he rolled on them, waving his paws in delight. If he heard any thoughts, they hadn't worried him.

'And why are you looking ill, my Jo Jo?' Dad asked.

I knew Sara was looking anxiously at me. 'Didn't Wendy tell you? I had a fall and went to hospital. Come on back – Mum's worried about Doddy. You should have said where you were going.'

'I wasn't going to tell that Wendy where I was taking him. I'm sure she's stopped your mum from contacting me.' I'd forgotten Dad's temper. His freckled face was red and his voice became really

Scottish. 'I'm going to give that lass a piece of my mind!'

'I don't think it was Wendy, really,' I began but he wasn't listening. That was my dad, charging like a big Highland bull into a situation without thinking.

Chapter 10

Once outside the Zoo, Dad insisted on ringing for a taxi from a phone box. 'Your mum'll be that worried,' he said.

'We'll get a bus,' Josh said.

'We can't pay,' Sara said flatly. 'I saw Josh empty his pocket to get in.'

'You'll come with us,' Dad said with a smile.

When the taxi came, Doddy started his usual crying at the sight of a car. 'No, no, no!' he yelled. 'Don't like cars. Don't drive, Dad.'

'That's silly,' Dad said. The taxi driver was looking impatient. 'You'll have to get over this, Donald,' Dad said but somehow he looked uncertain. 'The driver's really good and we'll not be going fast.'

'You went fast . . . very fast. Mum shouted *no Al – slow down*,' Doddy said. 'Then we went bang!'

'He means the accident. No – you got it wrong, Dods, Mum was driving, not Dad,' I said.

'He's got it right. I was driving,' Dad said in a low voice. Then he scooped Doddy up and we all bundled into the taxi, Doddy on Dad's knee. At first, my little brother's crying stopped us talking on the way back. Sara and Josh seemed numbed into silence by it all.

I went over and over what Dad had said. Somehow he'd let Mum take the blame for the accident. My dad – my big, strong dad who was so kind, always laughing, picked me up when I fell off my bike, taught me to swim, let me share his drum set, my dad had lied to get himself out of trouble.

'Why?' I asked him. 'Why did you lie about it?' I didn't care that Sara and Josh, squashed next to me in the taxi, were listening.

He looked over the top of Doddy's head at me. 'Yes, I drove that night. It was raining and I was going too fast. And Doddy . . .'

Doddy interrupted: 'Doddy went up, up, then down, bang!'

'Donald, be quiet,' Dad said. Doddy sucked his thumb. 'I could see Mum was in pain though Doddy seemed just to be shocked. There wasn't anyone in the parked van nor on the road so I said I'd walk to the nearest garage and telephone for an ambulance. Your mum said the police would come. You see, I was over the limit with the wine I'd drunk.' He stopped talking but I could read Sara's thoughts without the Eyes. She'd think Dad was just like her parents, always drinking.

'But you said you never drank and drove,' I said quickly.

He sighed and hugged Doddy. 'I can't think why I did – I never drink if I'm driving but I was so pleased to get the job. Well, she said if the police knew I was driving I'd be facing a charge of drunken driving and lose the new job. So she made me help her get out of the car – the front was half bashed in so we both had a job getting out of the car doors. She made me drag her round to the driver's seat. Doddy was half-conscious so he didn't know what happened. Later we found he'd had a bang on his head. I ran down the road and fetched help. The police arrived just as the ambulance men were taking your mum out of the car. Eventually, she got a caution for careless driving but of course, she'd not been drinking.'

'That wasn't fair on her,' Sara said suddenly.

'No – it wasn't,' Dad said. 'But we'd have had to sell the cottage if I'd been breathalysed because I'd probably have been suspended from driving for six months or more. And anyway no coach company is going to employ someone who's got a drunken driving conviction. So no more coach work for me.'

I thought of our little terraced cottage with its view over the fields to the sea. I supposed we'd have had to move to a tiny flat in some grotty estate. I began to see why Mum had done it but they'd both told lies, my mum and dad who were always banging on about being truthful. I felt sorry for them in a way. For the first time I thought it must be tough being grown-up.

Doddy started one of his tuneless chants, just like

he used to do, but the rest of us were silent until we arrived home.

Sara and Josh said they had to get back. I wished they hadn't listened to the embarrassing conversation in the taxi but at least I asked Dad for money to give to Josh for the Zoo tickets. Then the front door opened and Wendy stood there.

'So you found him,' she said. 'Why did you take him away, Alexander? Poor Lizzie's been so upset. You'd better come in.'

Mum met us in the hall. She dropped her stick and hugged Doddy. Then she stared at Dad.

'Sorry I worried you,' he said. 'Doddy said he had to go to the Zoo – so we went as you weren't there.'

'Didn't Wendy tell you I was collecting Jo from hospital?' Mum said.

'He didn't give me a chance to explain,' Wendy said.

'A tiger rolled on our eyes,' Doddy burbled.

'You've got a bit mixed up, darling,' Mum said, still hugging him. 'I think he's talking better, don't you, Al?'

'He's doing fine. So what's this about Jo and hospital?' Dad asked, putting his arm round me.

Wendy looked at my parents. I was impatient. Why couldn't they hug each other, not us, and make up so we could go home?

'I must go. I'm late for my Conference,' Wendy

said but suddenly, almost as if I had the Eyes again, I felt her sadness and loneliness flow round her like a dark cloak. She knew we might go now.

'Thank you for minding Doddy,' Mum said but she was already hurrying him down into our flat. I followed with Dad.

'So what happened to Jo?' he asked again when we were squashed onto the little sofa, Mum perching on the only other chair in the living room.

'She said she fell down some steps at school,' Mum began.

I thought it was time I told the truth for once so I explained.

Mum looked angry and Dad's face grew red. 'So the leader of this gang was that girl, who came back with us?' he exploded. 'If I'd known ... '

'It's over now. We're friends,' I said. 'Sara bullied people because she's unhappy at home. Her parents quarrel all the time. So I don't want to get her into any more trouble. After all, it was her mates who hurt me – and they're not likely to do much now without a leader.'

They both stared at me – I hoped they were thinking about their own quarrelling. I thought they might have said they'd make it up right now but Doddy said he was hungry, which reminded Mum that I hadn't had any lunch either. 'And you ought to go and rest. You've only just come out of hospital,' she said as we all drank tea and ate cheese sandwiches. Dad was looking at her as if he wanted to say something but couldn't make up his mind.

I couldn't just be sent to my room like a little kid without saying what I knew.

'Don't fuss, Mum. I'm OK,' I said. 'Isn't it time we talked about the accident?'

She was cutting her sandwich into small squares as if her life depended on it. 'That's all over. Water under the bridge.'

'Dad's told me what really happened. I wish you'd told me!' I burst out. 'I'm nearly thirteen. You could have told me the truth.'

'So you thought your father was a liar and made me take the blame?' Her hand was shaking as she stirred her tea, round and round – and she didn't take sugar.

'If you'd explained properly . . . but I don't see why you both quarrelled so much and why you took us away?' I tried to keep my voice calm because Doddy was staring, his cheeks bulging with sandwich.

Dad spoke at last. 'Jo – I felt guilty, see. And when you feel guilty you don't act normally. And I hated seeing your mum in pain because of me.'

'And I felt guilty too – lying to the police – and – well it all got too much so I got angry with your father. Can you understand that, Jo? I thought he'd be better on his own. Anyway, I shouldn't have let him have a drink if he was driving only we were so excited about the new job.'

'Doddy was bad. Did undo belt and jump about,' Doddy said suddenly.

'So that's what you were doing,' Dad said. 'It's true I was going too fast but I guess I might have avoided an accident, only all at once Doddy was bobbing about, blocking my view through the mirror and distracting me. It's confused in my mind now but I think I was going to pull out and overtake the parked van. Then a car I'd not seen overtook us at speed. That's when I went into the van.'

'I remember now,' Mum said slowly. 'Doddy was making a noise but I didn't realise he'd undone his belt. I thought afterwards that he fell into the passenger seat because the belt broke when we hit the van. Why didn't you tell me, Al?'

'I wasn't going to use Donald as an excuse. I was still driving too fast, my darling lass,' Dad said. 'And if I'd not drunk too much I'd have reacted quicker . . .'

'I'm sorry, Jo, about everything,' Mum said. 'But now you're older you must realise that grown-ups sometimes make bad mistakes.'

I nodded but my head hurt and suddenly it was all too much. I found I was crying and I couldn't stop. Then they were both comforting me. 'I want to go home!' I wailed like a little kid and Doddy joined in. 'Don't you love each other any more?'

99

There was a pause then they both said, almost together, 'Yes.' And it wasn't a lie. I could feel their love for each other as strong as the cloud of sadness that I'd felt round Wendy. The Eyes had left a little bit of magic behind or maybe I was growing up, as Mum said.

Chapter 11

'I am sorry you are going, Joanna,' said Morgan the Gorgon.

I couldn't believe it but she actually smiled. 'I was hoping you would enter our Art competition and sing in our school choir.' Well, she could have told me before!

I'd thought Dad would take us off then and there but of course life isn't like books. My parents spent ages talking when I'd gone to bed and it wasn't until the next day that Mum said we'd be going home after my dad's next coach trip.

So we stayed on at Grunge House for a while, with Wendy pretending to be happy for us and all the time puffing out clouds of loneliness. Mum said Wendy must come and stay but somehow, I knew it would never happen and I actually felt rather sad for poor Wendy.

Now Dad was borrowing Sandy's car and coming to fetch us the next day.

'You're needed by the Raving Rats,' Dad had told me. 'One of the Rats came to the door when I got back the first time and heard you'd all gone.' Dad looked away a moment as if he was remembering that terrible day. 'He left this note.'

I read: GET BAK SOON YOU PLONKAR WE NEED THE DRUMSET. MIKEY. His spelling wasn't any better than mine. So they hadn't forgotten me.

Now I said goodbye to the Gorgon and walked down the corridor for the last time. I met Lovey hurrying along to the gym. 'Best of luck, Joanna,' she said, smiling, and I knew I'd miss her.

I met Josh and Sara in the park after school. The Two Thugs had kept away from me lately. They'd heard about me going to hospital and I reckon they were dead scared I might still tell the whole story to the Gorgon. Sara and Josh seemed to have become mates and Sneaky must've been told off by the Gorgon because she laid off nagging Josh. None of the kids dared laugh at him for being a clever clogs with Sara there.

Doddy was still a bit scared of Sara so he hung back but Josh got him onto the roundabout. He and Sara pushed it gently and Doddy began one of his happy chants. I longed to go home and for us to be a family again but suddenly I knew I'd miss both of them and maybe even the school, as well.

There were only a few little kids around, maybe because it was windy, with great clouds racing across the sky. The big chestnut trees swayed and already the creamy blossom was falling and dimming into

102

brown piles on the damp ground. Funny how nothing stayed the same, I thought.

'Give us your address,' Sara said suddenly. 'I might send you a Christmas card or something.' I wrote it down and was surprised when Josh wanted it too.

'We go down to the West Country camping,' he said. 'Could take you too, Sara, if you want to come and your parents let you.'

I was gobsmacked when Sara went red and looked pleased.

Josh stood on his hands to make Doddy laugh. Then he righted himself. 'Remembered something,' he said and brought out a tatty bit of newspaper. He read it out loud:

'ZOO KEEPER SAYS HE'S A MIND READER

John Garnett (55), a keeper at Sevenstones Zoo, claims he can hear the animals' thoughts! John says, "I've helped Tim, our new tiger, and Ayesha, the elephant. They were moping and off their food. The animals told me what was wrong. Tim disliked being stared at and Ayesha wanted more space." The elephants are going to have a bigger enclosure and go out for a daily walk and a new, rocky den is being built at John's suggestion in the tiger enclosure, giving more privacy

103

to the animals. He says he is now following up complaints from one of the sealions who was tired of performing.

The Sevenstones Zoo Publicity Department declined to comment on Mr Garnett's communications with the animals but a spokesman said Mr Garnett had put forward some imaginative ideas for animal welfare. Sevenstones Zoo welcomed employees with initiative.'

Then there was some publicity about the Zoo conserving rare species.

'So the keeper found the Eyes and used them,' Josh said. 'I suppose they had to move the tigers if they just sat on the Eyes all the time.'

'I wonder how he cut out humans' thoughts,' I said.

'Maybe because he mainly thinks about animals,' Sara said.

'It was scary but it was sort of good for you. It made you feel not always in the centre of everything, hearing what other people thought,' I said.

'Yeah,' said Josh. 'I suppose the Eyes really are some kind of magic. They let you see or hear the truth about people.'

Sara said, 'It's scary, though. They're best with that keeper.'

I didn't tell them that I could sometimes still know what people were feeling. I wasn't sure they'd understand – perhaps I didn't myself.

Josh walked on his hands and Sara tried to copy him but kept falling over and giggling. Doddy tried to copy them and I just fell about laughing.

The wind blew the blossom off the trees like confetti. Summer was coming and life was great again.

RIVER of SECRETS

by Griselda Gifford

Fran is very upset because her mother has remarried and she has to live with her stepfather and his son at her gran's old home. She was very fond of her gran, who has recently been found dead in the nearby river. Was her death an accident? Fran is sure someone is to blame and she's determined to solve the mystery. Is the weird girl, Fay, who lives next door, hiding something? And why does another new friend, Denny, warn her against Fay's strange magic? Fran faces danger when the river almost claims a new victim, before she finally unlocks its secrets in a surprising and exciting climax to the story.

'A nail-biting novel' 4 star review, *Mizz Magazine*

ISBN 1842700456 £4.99